VOLUME THREE

AIRSHIP 27 PRODUCTIONS

Domino Lady-Volume Three

"Unbalanced" © 2019 Adam Mudman Bezecny
"Over a Barrel" & "Open Grave" © 2019 Gene Moyers
"The Domino Lady's Scandal" © 2019 Brad Mengel
"The Domino Lady Takes the Case" © 2019 Samantha Lienhard

Published by Airship 27 Productions
www.airship27.com
www.airship27hangar.com

Cover illustration © 2019 Ted Hammond
Interior illustrations © 2019 James Lyle

Editor: Ron Fortier
Associate Editor: Fred Adams Jr.
Marketing and Promotions Manager: Michael Vance
Production and design: Rob Davis.

ISBN-13: 978-1-946183-59-0
ISBN-10: 1-946183-59-8

Printed in the United States of America

10 9 8 7 6 5 4 3 2 1

Domino Lady

Volume Three
Table of Contents

UNBALANCED
By Adam Mudman Bezecny

The Domino Lady thought to herself: you know, it never is a good idea to have a gunfight in a cave.

First of all, there was really only one direction in which to go. Second, and more pressingly, guns were *loud*. To hear the stone sing back to her the tune of her glinting silver .22 was a cacophony beyond reckoning. Still, if she didn't take her shot, there was no way she was going to catch her quarry. What a predicament. The woman up ahead of her, the brunette called Janice Smart, lived up to her name and packed her ears with earplugs. She was the boldest jewel thief the Domino Lady had ever set herself to.

The young, lithe blonde didn't miss a beat in charging after the darker-haired woman. At her feet was the soft sand of the beach cave she'd followed Smart into. The gun-blast she unleashed lit the way, but only for a moment. Even with the pain searing in her ears, and the darkness ahead of her, she kept on, like a bloodhound made hominid. She'd been in this business too long for a little pain and a little dark to make a fool out of her. Smart had worn her earplugs for a reason—she was shooting back at her pursuer.

The Domino Lady was also quite accustomed to evading bullets at this point, but in such a tight-hugging space it was a hard feat to pull off. She just had to count on Lady Luck, and while they were old friends, Lady Luck was never kind even to her closest friends. She let off a silent prayer nonetheless, banking on their sharing of a noble title to stand in for a favor. It turned out Luck liked other Ladies, as every bullet was nothing but a zing and a rush of wind. She only wondered when they were going to run out of cave.

There were so many questions, ringing in her head along with the tinnitus. Why was Smart so desperate to get away with the jewels she'd taken that she was willing to shoot at her? Why had she abstained from using weapons in her previous robberies? What was she possibly hoping to achieve by leading her into this cave?

A possible answer to that last question was that it made for easy disposal of the body. If this passage kept going, it probably opened up into pits somewhere. Maybe Smart was a secret killer; maybe she just hid the bodies of those she killed and that's why she was never suspected of murder. The only way for the Domino Lady to find out would be to catch her.

As she predicted, the cavern opened up. Another gunshot confirmed they were now roaming in a wider room. The orange light of Smart's gun revealed there were hidden perils of this fresh space, including several of the prophesied pits. It was almost suicide to keep going, but the Domino Lady had never failed yet. The woman behind the black mask, who stared out through the vigilante's eyes, had to remember that. Ellen Patrick was the delight of parties but she never forgot the thrum of hunting criminals, like the criminals who had killed her father. If there was even a slight chance that Janice Smart was a killer, she would be put down like the mad dog she was. For what she'd done already, she'd leave in handcuffs at the very least.

The pouch of the top of her sheer black garter contained her trademark syringe of knockout drugs, but it didn't have a flashlight. Something to remember for future cases, then. But in the dark she heard the click of a pistol dead ahead—a sign of the emptiness of the burglar's gun. Then, faintly, Smart cursed. Those noises revealed where she was, and with this opportunity ahead of her, the Domino Lady dove in with the precision of a homing missile.

Her tight body smacked hard against warm flesh. Nails struggled against her flesh in the dark; then, those nails were joined by teeth. Stifling a grunt of pain, the Domino Lady reeled back, and Smart shoved her off onto the hard stone. Then she was back on her feet, and heavy footsteps carried her way. But Ellen wasn't short-winded, either, and with twice her prior speed she dashed off again.

Now it looked like the darkness was breaking. She squinted her eyes, and pinched her face tight, trying to remain stoic in the face of this shining brightness—but it was an orange light, not from gunfire but from candlelight. Immediately the question of oxygen supply entered her mind; but that was inquisitive Ellen Patrick asking the question. The Domino Lady was wondering what the hell Smart was doing in a place lit by candles. Torches, more properly—she could see them now. Her eyes struggled at first to adjust to the change in light, but that, too, was something she'd made her body a mistress of.

Where had Smart got to? She could see now via the torches that the stone passage was ordered into rows of stacked bricks. The tunnel this formed veered off ahead, twisting into a corner which had evidently swallowed Smart. But when she rounded this corner, there was no sign of her target, even though this passage went on unbending for a while. It was alarming at first to the Domino Lady. The dark passage, lit with wide-ly-spaced torches, led out somewhere—into another great opening, even larger in scale than the open area they'd passed through. She took a few cautious steps forward, trying to see what it was that awaited her in that enormous room. It was almost like there was a statue, in the shape of an enormous man, whose feet could be seen. Yet she couldn't help but feel that it was a man at all. It was the statue of a colossal *woman*...

That feeling of strangeness intensified. A fear ached at the back of her mind that Janice Smart was a ghost. At once it seemed like that ghost reared up at her and screamed in her face. She felt a brief sense of nausea and lost consciousness.

When Ellen Patrick opened her eyes, her eyelids felt the weight of the domino mask, the black of which, along with her dress's white, supplied her the title of Domino Lady. She was relieved that her captors had left her mask on. She knew that there were "captors" in this situation because her wrists were tightly bound with a thick cord. From how things felt it seemed she had her hands behind her, keeping her trapped in a chair.

Her vision cleared at a painfully slow rate. Several figures surrounded her, but they didn't make any sudden moves—through the fog she could see that some of them were smiling. That made this situation infinitely worse. It was never good to see your enemies *smiling* at you, especially if they were in a dark underground settlement lit with ornamental torches.

God, she hadn't seen before that the torches were stylized—probably because of the drugged gas that had doubtlessly lined that passage. She couldn't recognize them perfectly but there were runic marks on the hold-ers of the torches, as well as some carved into the wood itself. Faintly, she had the impression these were alchemist's symbols—occult signs. Perhaps the horde of women crowded around were some sort of devil-cult. They were all clad in scarlet robes, which helped set the imagery perfectly.

"I suppose next you'll drug me again and put on the altar to Father Dagon," the Domino Lady joked weakly.

"There'll be no such thing," came a voice ahead of her (her vision had still not yet become perfect). "You know, for a very long while, you were at the top of our recruitment list."

"It's an honorable placement." Another voice spoke now—also female.

All of the people here were women. There were some who looked to have manly jaws and faces, but to the Domino Lady's eyes they were women. "Presently you are still in our top five, alongside Maria Flores, Linda Turner, Kyra Zelas, and Tara Obongo, so the offer is an open one."

"Why would I join your organization if I don't even know what it is?"

One woman in particular stepped forth out of the crowd. She looked to Ellen to be Japanese in appearance, but she also seemed to be a blend of many races. Her face was sharp, intelligent, and hard. Her hair was dark, but the longer the Domino Lady looked at it, the more it seemed to contain more colors besides black and brown; this strange effect remained even when she was sure her vision was restored to normalcy. She grinned broadly at her captive as she set a single hand on her hip.

"This is the Order of the Madonna," she explained. "We are a group of women dedicated to the cause of protecting and fighting for women all over the world. As you may anticipate from what our Jan has been up to, we sometimes fund these operations with goods we take from the hands of others. We attempt to steal exclusively from Western institutions built with the cruelty of empire, which has earned us a harsh reputation among certain voices in the media."

"You've been condemned for stealing? I can't imagine why. Are these 'certain voices' in the media the people you've robbed?"

"Some of them, yes—others are third parties who are simply concerned about the ideological affront to the idea of personal property. But it's worth noting that behind the scenes, some of them object to us because we are taking away their slaves. We take from them the bodies of women they purchased, as if they were furniture. They don't like us taking the ones they beat, the ones they keep pregnant, and out of schools. They seem respectable to the public, sometimes, when they write about us, and people buy it when it's their pen on the paper. Does any of that strike you as an ounce familiar?"

The Domino Lady mulled over these words...they had a point. Women had only gotten the right to vote within her lifetime. She remembered being a child and hearing about it on the radio, and thinking, however briefly, about what that meant for her future, little understanding at the time that she shouldn't take it for granted.

"There is a reason we wanted to recruit you, Ms. Patrick," spoke the strange-haired woman.

The Domino Lady was taken aback, but replied, with missing a beat: "You know who I am then, eh? Even without a peek under the mask."

"Oh, yes. As I said, we have been studying you. Janice's gunplay in the caves was a final test of your physical abilities. We're pleased to see that they match the other attributes of your body." At this the women laughed, and Ellen saw that Janice Smart was among them. She didn't join in their laughter.

"Let her go!" called a voice from the back, and this was seemingly taken as an edict. They came forward and cut the ropes that bound her, though they kept her wrists clasped together, at least at first. They let her go, to her mild surprise, and she could feel she retained her syringe and gun. But it would be foolish to try to blast her way out, and there was no chance of a hand-to-hand victory against this many people, especially when many of them looked fit. She could believe that these were women accustomed to field missions with an element of danger involved.

She had been tied up at the back of a small alcove, which led out into a larger expanse. At their left, now, the Domino Lady could see the idol which she had glimpsed earlier; the vigilante recalled pictures she'd seen in college of the old Akkadian sculptures of Ishtar. For all she knew this *was* Ishtar—a goddess of love and femininity. Or perhaps it was Aphrodite of the Greeks, or Venus of the Romans. In all probability these were all just faces of the same deity, at least from a certain point of view. This figure towered about a dozen feet tall, and her hands were out before her in some sort of prayer. Her eyes had a quiet dignity about them.

"Maybe I'd be more assured of your interests if you told me what you actually *did*. It's one thing to say that you go around the world helping women, but you need to back that up with evidence. What was one of your operations?"

"You recall back about ten years ago, in 1928—the Princess of Graustark was kidnapped by the Grisson Gang during her ambassadorial trip to New York. The Grisson Gang are infamous torturers of women," said her nameless hostess.

"I remember. And that's not a bad description for them. They were bold enough to think they could sell her into slavery."

"And they nearly succeeded, too. Perhaps you've had a chance to read the documents about how extensive their operation was in those days— they've diminished now even if their fangs haven't yet dulled."

"You're saying you stopped them?"

"They and the ring they were 'trading' with. The Princess went back to Graustark safe as houses. And this—" She paused, then, to produce a long, gray cord.

She didn't finished before the Domino Lady cried out: "That's part of the regal uniform of the Graustark monarchy!"

"You are well-versed in politics."

"I try to keep up on things," the adventuress laughed. "Let me see that." And she looked the ribbon over. "That's the Graustark sash, alright. Of course, you could have stolen it, but I know a liar when I hear one. You seem on the level to me."

"We are honored to have earned the trust of the Domino Lady," her hostess said.

"And what should I call you?"

"There is a name you may know me by, which is a name of horror for many. Long will my exploits be told by those who didn't understand my aims. I won't speak that horror-name to you, so instead, you may call me by the name of the dream-demoness who inspired the hated title I normally walk in. To you, I am called Smarra."

The Domino Lady crossed her arms, but retained her bemusement. "That's certainly a roundabout way of telling me a name. Are you still offering me a job, then...'Smarra'?"

"Do you want the job?"

"No."

"Then that is a pity, but we have no qualm. Consent is paramount to our Order."

The conversation lapsed, but the Domino Lady arched her eyebrow. Her curiosity was getting the better of her, as it always did.

"Why did you choose to contact me at just this moment? Was it a coincidence? You just happened to be stealing on my turf?"

Smarra's eyebrow mirrored Ellen's. "I was hoping you would ask. The truth of it is that we were hoping you'd join us in our present operation. You see, that's why we stole the jewelry that we did—it's the last of a nest egg we're packing together while conducting our current intelligence investments."

"Meaning?"

"Meaning that one of our trademark schemes has gone awry, as it does from time to time. You see, we do try to avoid stealing. But sometimes, our members will go out and marry wealthy men, and, in essence, embezzle them."

"I see." The Domino Lady was not averse to using the robbery of rich men to cover the expenses of her work.

"However, we take care to choose men whose riches are ill-gotten. We want to punish those who victimize people along lines of class, and who go after women, specifically. Among them have numbered noblemen like the wicked Duke Blangis, and Christian, Lord Kelso. The Prouse fortune has served us well—you'd like Prouse. He is or was a fellow adventurer, and I think the two of you use the same brand of knockout drugs in your needles. In any case, the most recent addition to our little family was a scientist generally perceived as a crackpot by the name of Dr. Jilderay Norse. We understood that he was something of a woman-hater, but he took to his wife well enough to marry her. Much to our chagrin, his wife ended up failing somewhat in her mission, and he learned what we were planning to do to him. Whether the thought of losing his considerable inheritance exposed his inner nature, or if fear twisted him into what he is today, he became dedicated to being totally antithetical to our cause. An unfortunate prejudice common to our time became a deep-seated, bloodthirsty hatred. Dr. Norse became obsessed with the idea of creating a global order where women exist exclusively as men's slaves. He set himself up as a criminal under the lurid alias of Bluebeard."

The Domino Lady turned away from her, and paced away from the crowd, her white dress swaying behind her. To her bemusement, she could feel more than a few sets of eyes watching her figure—which were not entirely unwelcome. "Bluebeard—has he ever killed women?"

"Well, none that were married to him. But yes. He and his crew have taken hostages, and while we've used our pull and coin to fight them on that front, they haven't always stayed true to their word. Bluebeard's as vicious as his namesake—moreso. In each of his lairs we've found, there's been a room just for torturing and killing women, like in the fairy tale. But Bluebeard had just one secret abattoir. Perhaps it would be better to call him Blackbeard for all he's done."

The Domino Lady pursed her lips. "Can he do it? I mean, can he create this sort of...hyper-patriarchy, on a worldwide scale?"

"Well, that's just the thing. He was a crackpot scientist, as I said—and his interests involved extraterrestrial contact."

"Wait...aliens? Like that Orson Welles show a few weeks back?"

"I'm afraid so. It seems Dr. Norse's little order, or counter-order, was able to make contact with a race of beings from goddess-knows-where. We don't know what these creatures look like, but we're sure they exist. With the aid of these beings, Dr. Norse has created a device of supreme power."

"What kind of power?"

"That's what our investments have been for. We've long desired to inspect this device firsthand. If we were to supply you with the proper information, we believe that you could do some serious damage."

She sighed, but also laughed. "Even if this is all even somewhat true—why me? We keep dodging around the topic of why you want to recruit me."

"Because you are a woman."

Smarra came up behind her and ran a hand down the back of her neck, which came to settle on the soft skin of her shoulder, rendered smooth now that the November goose-pimples were gone. It was strangely warm in this cave. "The Order of the Madonna believes that there must be balance between the male and the female, animus and anima. For millennia, we have been off-balance. Our Order exists to restore that balance, and to prevent the balance from being broken."

The Domino Lady nodded at this.

"Dr. Norse is operating out of Los Angeles. He has a base near the ports. Will you help us?"

Ellen Patrick thought of the world in flames—all of her friends, in chains, to be used and abused as men saw fit.

"Let's do it."

"Yes, let's. You and me." Smarra stepped in front of her now. "I am the Madonna of this Order, and I'll join you in the fray."

"Sounds like a rare honor."

Smarra danced her eyes across Ellen's shoulder just as she'd danced her hand across it. "Trust me, you have no idea."

Smarra and several of her bodyguards took the Domino Lady up an elevator to the top of the hill under which their temple was buried, and when they emerged they found a car already waiting for them. The vigilante wondered how all of this was possible, which was a question intensified by where the car brought them. They were swiftly deposited on the grounds of an extensive airport, where a private helicopter was primed for takeoff. It traveled at speeds swifter than what the adventuress thought possible for such vehicles—but it didn't seem to matter to her somehow. The Order of the Madonna seemed to be quite rich, and perhaps that accounted for it. It wasn't long before the lights of LA were up before them, and they came in for a landing.

That was when the bodyguards left them. They had traveled silently. Once her guards were gone, however, the woman who called herself the Madonna turned to her compatriot, and spoke softly.

"We're going to have to use maximal stealth from here on out. It's not ideal that you're wearing white, but I recognize the symbolism you carry."

"And it hasn't steered me wrong." The vigilante surveyed the landscape. "I get the impression we're aiming for that tunnel over there...it looks like it's part of the sewer drainage."

"Correct. The tunnel has been deemed obsolete by the city...a few years back they replaced it with a new drain elsewhere. They never demolished the tunnel, despite safety complaints. Needless to say, the Order wondered why that was."

"So I take it you followed a money line at some point."

"Yes. It's still so very easy to bribe people in this country, especially politicians. That tunnel will look abandoned for some time but I suspect we'll swiftly have to deal with guards."

"Someone's got to sort out the kids who are going to stick their necks in there," the masked detective sighed. She wondered how many teens had gone mysteriously missing in these parts. In a place like LA their cases would end up buried under so many others.

They dropped back to silence, and advanced on the tunnel. The moon was full over the waters of the Pacific, and it was like a fluttering sheet of diamonds on the surface of an unending pool of ink. The dim lights of the city were like campfires on the prairies, perched here and there on the mute rocky fingers of the skyline. It was easy to believe that the entire city was just an ancient ruin, cold and quiet and dead. Entering the tunnel only worsened the feeling—it was like walking into the entrance to a sepulcher. Except all the religious iconography that made such a thing holy, regardless of faith, was scrubbed clean by years of water flow, reduced now to crude and incomprehensible graffiti. The standing water, which doubtlessly bred mosquitoes in the summer, pooled from the drip of the meager rains which replaced the snows blanketing the rest of the country at this time. The November chill was once more harsh to the Domino Lady, but she showed no sign of the cold. One might think she was trying to seem impressive in front of the authoritative Madonna, who now walked so effortlessly into this place of danger, but this was not the case—truthfully, Ellen Patrick cared little for the opinions of anybody anymore. She walked in a different world, and for nothing less than her own standard she didn't shiver in the damp cold of the tunnel.

"That tunnel will look abandoned…"

Like the cave which had led to the den of the Order of the Madonna, this tunnel, geometrically hewn in a stark contrast to the tectonic roughness of its counterpart, grew warmer the deeper in they went. This was explained in part when Ellen, now in the lead, rounded the next corner. Her shadow passed in front of the blazing lights of an electric lamp, which carried with them the warmth of voltage. There were several of them spaced throughout the corridor that greeted those who turned this corner, all crudely strung along on power cables stemming farther back into the passage. The Domino Lady paused to cast a shadowed look back at Smarra, and the two shared a significant glance. Someone was definitely hiding himself down here, and it was an easy feat—aside from the dripping precipitation at the entrance, this tunnel was bone-dry. Smarra's info was right: it hadn't been used for its intended purpose for quite some time.

They continued down, entering a loop of corners that had them crossing back underneath where they had first entered. The floor beneath them became the pounding metal slats of a steel catwalk. They were up above an open space, which was lit from far below by more of the electrical lamps from the passageway. The Domino Lady looked up, and she could practically feel the strain of the stone above them as it held up the sea. It was too dark to see the roof of this new space properly, and she wondered if there was any reinforcement at all to hold the water back. She was usually prepared for most things but this was entirely unexpected. Before they could probe too far, however, there came the sound of rushing footsteps below them.

They stopped, realizing only now that their own footsteps were echoing down. All the same, they did not seem to be detected at first. There were galloping wolves in human form straight below them. Soldiers. Never a good sign, especially when one was below the ocean—and so close to a major city. A million thoughts flashed through the Domino Lady's mind. Maybe they were Germans, or Japanese. But it was more likely that Dr. Jilderay "Bluebeard" Norse had gone even farther in expanding his territory than the Order of the Madonna had once thought. He had acquired enough of a fortune to hire mercenaries as formidable as the Marines. These soldiers were wearing strange bootleg editions of ordinary U.S. military outfits, and the rifles they held were the same sort of Thompsons that gangsters like the Grisson Gang were fond of. These men weren't simple Camonte Mob hired guns, though—they meant business. As the Domino Lady's eyes traced them out, she also observed that, down at the chamber's bottom, there were lines of tanks set out casually like cars at a parking garage.

This wasn't just an idle cult. This was a violent military force, ready to subvert democracy at any moment—all in the name of shoving down people who were already shoved down to begin with.

It made her sick, and she could feel an angry buzz in the air from Smarra sharing that sentiment with her. Ellen once more reached for her weapons, never taken from her. She considered opening a burst of shots, but the second one of those dragon's maws they were carrying turned its fire on her she was a dead woman. Best to just keep moving along the cat-walk, and save her bullets.

Eventually the metal walkway linked up again with another labyrinth of corridors and the vigilante and Smarra passed down a staircase into more comfortable accommodations—the hallway here was rather like one which one might find in a hotel, and now the walls were lined with doors. The first on their right was slightly ajar, and it was Smarra who pointed this fact out to the detective. She raised a shushing finger to her lips as she opened it, but the Domino Lady went first, drawing her gun. As she faced it out before her, she surveyed that she wouldn't need it for now—this room, an office, was empty. There was a lamp on the table which had been left on, however, suggesting the owner might come back soon. Once they were both inside they reset the door to its original position, and Ellen whispered: "I think maybe we can take a hostage."

"That's what I was thinking. We just have to be—"

Someone heard the whispers. Prejudicial thought had ruined them, the Domino Lady realized. They had gone in here anticipating dull fools—the usual proponents of woman-hating. They had seen a pack of burly male soldiers and presumed everyone in this facility to be a brainless thug. But down here, the men Bluebeard had hired had trained ears, and they were closer than the Domino Lady and her companion had expected. Still, there was nothing the Domino Lady wasn't prepared for. Three men appeared suddenly, knocking the door back hard against the wall. One of them had an assault rifle, but he was at the back—the other had a pistol, and the last had a knife. The guy with the pistol was the most threatening, but if she dropped him then Mr. Machine-Gun would be up in his place. Her first action was nearly automatic. Her pistol was in her hand, her finger was pulling the trigger, and the bullet was about to strike his gun. In an instant he dropped the weapon, and when he dove low to search for it, the Domino Lady was already in his face. She slammed an uppercut into him which drove him up and backwards. He was still her little meat-shield against the guy with the big rifle.

This left her flank wide open for Sir Knife, but Smarra had marked him in her mind. She strode forward confidently, with a mind on her form, and with a single blow from her strong hand she rendered the man's neck bruised and his mind unconscious. For all the Domino Lady knew, he was dead. The pistol-man was starting to put himself back together, and while he shook off the pain in his jaw he reached to his belt, where he produced a saber whose hilt had previously blended in with the rest of his uniform. He gave a ferocious cry, muted somewhat by the scarlet bruises erupting out where her fist had connected. She punched him again, in the gut this time, and threw him back on the man with the machine-gun.

She wasn't expecting him to try to shoot her *through* his friend. There was a quieted burst of gunfire which ended the life of the pistol-man.

The Domino Lady was spared both the incoming bullets and the sight of awful carnage by the timely motion of Smarra. The Madonna shoved her out of the way, knocking down onto the floor. The twice-punched man fell sloppily off of the man with the rifle, his entire form now limp butter. The shooter was undeterred, even though he was now covered in blood. He was going to shoot the two of them down till the Domino Lady remembered she was holding a gun of her own. Still she aimed just for the gun; at this range she could get a slug right down his barrel. He knew already that if he fired, his plans would go up in his face, like fireworks. With a single slick motion, she drew her narcotic needle and lunged forward, plunging the syringe deep into his calf.

In a moment, it was over, and he was unconscious. She staggered upward, trying to remain optimistic, despite the fatalities. That was that for her knockout drugs, and, unless Smarra had given her a reload when she was out, most if not all of her bullets. Not great condition, for the start of an operation. But she'd left her trademark purse behind when she'd set out after Smart, the jewel thief, and that had her spare vials and ammo.

She was glad not to be alone in a moment like this. She saw now that the man Smarra had attacked was squirming and groaning, though he wouldn't be up again for a long while—she'd managed to avoid lethal force. "You handled yourself beautifully out there," she told the Madonna.

The Domino Lady looked over her hostess in depth for the first time. She was a very petite sort of woman--not short, but with a small frame, so that she seemed to have something of a large head. But that head was very beautiful, olive-skinned, with deep dark eyes and high cheekbones. Her black hair (which sometimes seemed red or even blonde depending on the lighting) was long and wild, and highlighted her curving shoulders perfectly. Her body's outline was apparent below the sweeping red ceremonial robes she wore, which reached down to her boot-clad ankles. Shrouded below her tangled hair was a hood, of the same sort which her followers had used to shadow their faces.

"The poet Romain Ravillac dedicated an entire poem to my fighting routine. It was perhaps the most romantic set of lines he wrote me, before his unfortunate demise," Smarra said. "I believe it was called 'The War-Dance of Astarte.' An apt title, I think."

They silently decided to move onward—they'd stopped this pack of guards before they could call up any sort of alarm, but this place was more heavily populated than they'd first thought. At this point they *were* trying to impress each other: who could move more quietly? The Domino Lady's white dress made her look like a ghost against the uncanny shadows of this place, while Smarra's crimson form seemed unearthly somehow, as if she really was the ethereal Madonna she claimed herself to be.

But no amount of silence could hide them from what awaited them next. There was such little light in this place that it was tough to foresee what sort of menaces awaited them. Ellen heard the low growl up ahead, but couldn't associate it with anything—it could've been the low hum of a radiator. Yet, no such luck. Though there were other outlets, the passage ended with a long stretch of tight bars that formed the outline of a dog kennel. Inside were several large mastiffs, ordinarily such tame beasts, but now starved or reared to hatefulness. At once the Domino Lady considered there was nearly something gendered in this, as well. Dogs were always considered *man's* best friend—in the dog/cat dichotomy, dogs were masculine and cats feminine. She wondered then if the Order of the Madonna kept an army of tigers or lions. But she didn't want to play to stereotype. It was enough that these dogs were killers, and the vigilante was struck with a rare bout of fear, even though in the bustle of daytime parties, Ellen Patrick was often accompanied by dogs. Ellen had always preferred big dogs like these, who so reminded her of the hunting dogs her father kept in her youth.

And so it was that she couldn't bring herself to hurt these dogs, which was perhaps a boomeranged advantage. Those slobbering jaws could take her arm off if they got to it, but even that didn't deter her from pacifism. "Run, Smarra!" she urged, but the Madonna held her ground. She was going to try to fight these beasts, with no worries about the risks to herself.

Ellen had spotted, even through the darkness, that the doors to these kennels had been opened remotely; she hoped one of the nearby passages would lead into whatever room controlled that door. At the root of every bad dog was a worse owner. She wanted to hand that owner's own head back to him, with two black eyes on top of everything.

More and more hooks to these hallways—Dr. Norse evidently fancied himself a new Daedalus. But Ellen kept her wits about her, and surely, in the space behind where the dogs were kept, there was a room with a large control panel set into the wall linked to that which joined the kennel. She wondered what the other controls were for—perhaps something to help boost the violent tendencies of the dogs, through the delivery of pain, no doubt. There was a man who was shirtless save for a scrappy vest of some variety, who was eyeing the controls with a grin on his face. He turned around and at once his biceps puffed up. Even before Ellen arrived he'd been slathered with a thin layer of sweat.

"I don't like what you do to women, or to dogs," the Domino Lady said to him.

"What's the difference?" was his reply.

She spat at him, and at that, his face twisted to a visage of rage. He snarled at her like one of his tormented dogs and came towards her. She was ready for him, wishing she still had a needle full of tranqs. She settled for the tranquilizing properties of her fists and legs, full of justified fury.

The big man put up a good fight—in all fairness, he was a good two heads taller than the costumed adventuress, and the muscles in his arms were just about as big as her head. The secret of course was just that she never let him hit her. Sometimes her jabs were light—sometimes he got real dumb about the angles and she could get in stronger blows. She mostly aimed for the head, but there wasn't much within his skull, so it took a great deal of these hits before he started looking seriously winded. Sluggishness struck her, too, but only briefly—a flashback came upon her once again to the days of her old mastiffs. There had been one she'd really liked, who'd died when she was very, very young...what was his name again? What had Dad's bad sense of humor dreamed up for him...?

Oh yeah. "Hard-Biter."

That was the knockout hit, and the big brute slumped over backwards. In an ideal world his dogs would now be free of pain—but the Domino Lady knew that when it came to these things, like these terrorist organizations, it was foolish to hope sometimes.

Smarra entered the room then, and the Domino Lady observed at once that there wasn't a mark on her. There were no external blood-stains, either, rendering how she handled those dogs a mystery. Ellen didn't want to ask questions. Wordlessly, Smarra pointed back into the network of hall-ways. They had to keep moving.

The corridor snaked up ahead, and there were several plaques on the wall with arrows indicating what awaited them. The Domino Lady point-ed significantly at the plaque reading, "Hangar." It had been enough to see the tanks, but to consider that there were aircraft as well was a disturbing prospect. All the other destinations appeared to be more dormitories and office spaces, which likely crawled with personnel. Not like a hangar was likely to be abandoned, but it would be less cramped, a better scene if more shooting came into the picture. Ellen just counted her lucky stars that the previous gunshots, and the barking of the dogs, hadn't tipped yet more people off.

When they steered themselves into the hangar, they found themselves as they had before, on a catwalk high above the aircraft. However, there was a ladder by which they could access the hangar floor, if they wanted to—and something told them they really didn't want to. Hordes of men were tending to a neat set of helicopters of extremely modern makes, rivals of the Madonna's own vehicle. It was the configuration of these choppers, however, that caught the eye of the Domino Lady. They were arranged so as to carry the large, heavy-looking net that was spread in the middle of their ring. It looked like they were planning to use these whirlybirds to carry something of tremendous weight. Observing further, the vigilante could see that the "floor" the fleet sat on was actually an enormous hatch—the level of power that would be necessary to pull back those great doors only added to the marvel of the scale of this place.

Slowly, her mind assembled more and more sense out of the hangar's layout. Now she comprehended the large tower structure at the far left of the room, which extended, with something of a gap, past the enormous doors that constituted the chamber's bottom. A hatch at the tower's base could open independently of the main gates, and if she interpreted the mechanisms at the top of the tower correctly, which seemed to have the capacity to extend outward, the structure's primary purpose was for drop-ping heavy cargo into this huge net carried by the helicopters. To find out what this cargo was, they would need to go downward. At the base of the shaft was likely a lift used to carry it to this level.

Without thinking, the Domino Lady went to the ladder. Behind her, however, Smarra whispered, "Wait!"

She froze. She wondered if the Madonna was afraid—if she was, it was a strange thing. But Ellen Patrick had also been the Domino Lady long enough to know that fear and apprehension were easily mistaken for one another by a less intelligent portion of society.

"Dr. Norse is down there," Smarra said.

"How do you know?"

"Can't you feel it in the air? This chamber is where his plan culminates. Those men are tending to the helicopters rather frantically, aren't they? Whatever's being loaded into that net is being launched *soon*..."

"You're right. But that doesn't mean—"

"Hear me out, my sister. I can tell from your words that you lack a certain intuition to these things, which I entirely comprehend. But here the scales of the cosmos—that balance between the forces—is shifted. It's almost *mystical*..."

"Now, look, Smarra, I've had some weird run-ins over the years, but I'm not sure I believe this. It sounds like something out of some mentalist show with the Great Stanton or Professor Leonide or some such. But what I'll say is this: if Bluebeard is at the bottom of this chamber, then I'm bringing him in."

Smarra held her tongue. Privately, she knew that the Domino Lady would not believe her talk about what was presently happening between dimensions.

The two of them went down as quietly and as stealthily as they could. They knew their crimson and white garments would stand out if they were spotted, so the trick was to not be spotted. It was a long and treacherous climb down, but when they at last reached the bottom, they found there was a lighted alcove nearby, and within this alcove was a hatch such as that seen on submarines.

Ellen turned the hatch's wheel slowly, keeping one eye cast back over her shoulder. There was no hiding the sound of the hatch, but by now they were testing the rotors of the chopper fleet, which kept the soldiers preoccupied. Once it was opened she hurriedly urged Smarra to enter, and she followed. The change in air pressure suggested to her that they were in yet another hallway.

But it was only a stub of one. There was just one door here, off to the left, which led into an ominous orange candlelight. Like cats, they stole into this room, and saw it was an office, nearly identical to the one where they had nearly been ambushed. It was not abandoned—no matter how silent they were, they'd walked right into a meeting.

The Domino Lady knew which one was Bluebeard, though the large beard he bore was not blue—Blondbeard, if it wasn't already taken, was not a charming epithet. His eyes were wild beneath his thick glasses, and his hunched form was draped in a white labcoat. The hands which were pointing at the sheaf of papers scattered across his desk looked to be dipped in thick, rubbery oil, forming the dark gloves which masked the flesh of his digits.

And yet the Domino Lady could recognize Dr. Jilderay Norse for reasons beyond his facial hair, and stereotypically scientific appearance. He was, aside from the two women, the only one in the room who was human. At the scientist's sides were a number of creatures which appeared to be oversized hominid mantises. Their staring orange eyes formed isolated islands in the alien green carapace, wrapped over the shape of something inscrutably inhuman with long, nasty looking front legs. Ellen drew her gun, but she had too few shots to blast all these creatures. Smarra stepped ahead of her and waved her hand gently, as if she could somehow dismiss all of this with a gesture.

"Do not be alarmed by the appearance of the Zha-gai Insects," Norse pronounced. "They are far from being native to Earth, it's true, but it would be far from the first time Earth made contact with extraterrestrials. They are scholars, thaumaturges, and nobility is in their blood—they are rather like the philosopher-kings of whom Plato wrote. We automatically view them as animals but they are far beyond us."

"So you did succeed in contacting aliens," Smarra replied.

"You take the news well, witch-queen," Norse said. "Neither of us anticipated how easily I would find a race sympathetic to my interests. The Zha-gai are more than willing to assist me in my efforts to create a utopia where the proper way of things in matter of gender is restored." He cut himself off before explaining further. "Who is this scantily-clad trollop you've brought with you?" Despite the harshness of his words, it was quite clear he was examining Ellen's figure, with his eyes lingering in key areas.

"I'm the Domino Lady," Ellen said simply.

"And I didn't bring her with me, she brought me with her," Smarra said humbly.

"I'm decently impressed with your operation," the Domino Lady said, speaking honestly. "But speaking as a lady, I don't take too kindly to a world where I'm someone's slave. Where *anyone* is anyone's slave. So even if you've got some big bugs on your side, we're stopping this here and now."

Dr. Norse took a while to reply. At first his face was that of a statue. Then, it split with a grin, and he threw his head back to laugh. "That's pretty good," he said. "But unfortunately, I will always have the advantage. The powers the Zha-gai command are beyond your comprehension. Consider, for example, the fact that I was able to hear you up above when the Madonna started talking about balance. The words 'microphone' and 'speaker' would be inadequate to describe the devices I used to listen in on you."

"So you could hear us chat. What does that matter?" asked the Domino Lady.

"Well, the mention of balance is significant, you oddly-garbed creature. Let me explain as I retract these panels, and show off the main chamber." He gestured to the wall opposite his office's entrance, and at the seeming motion of his hands, the walls began to slide apart. Ellen observed that the so-called "Zha-gai" were now moving their limbs slightly, as if straining themselves—evidently it was by their power that the walls moved. Dr. Norse said: "Since the time of the Greeks, and since the conception of heliocentrism, humans have theorized that there was another world on the opposite side of the sun almost identical to our own. They have called this planet the Counter-Earth, and from that name, some have speculated that this world forms some sort of cosmic axis with our Earth that keeps everything in balance. This stands in contradiction to the prevailing idea that balance is essential, as in the balance between the genders. One opposite must always rule the other. Now, clearly, whichever Counter-Earth is joined to ours presently is of feminine alignment. This means the balance is shifted towards the unnatural state of womanhood reigning supreme. The recent appearance of suffragettes and other menaces to society were the first signs of a counter-natural order taking control—the Order of the Madonna, meanwhile, is a sign that this Counter-Earth's energies are leeching deep into our native soil. This must be averted or the world will be wracked with dozens of calamities—earthquakes, fires, tornadoes, and God above knows what else."

"Hold on...what?" The Domino Lady's voice was loud and booming. "That doesn't even *come close* to making sense! What do you mean, 'feminine alignment'? And your phrasing implies there's, what, more than one Counter-Earth? It stands in complete defiance to all modern astronomical knowledge."

"It's difficult to explain," Norse confessed. "But it makes sense, I assure you. The Counter-Earth exists on another dimensional plane of existence. Each planet possesses a sort of gendered energy. Venus has female energy, as you may expect, while Mars has masculine energy. Occasionally our Earth forms a dimensional bond with one specimen out of the variety

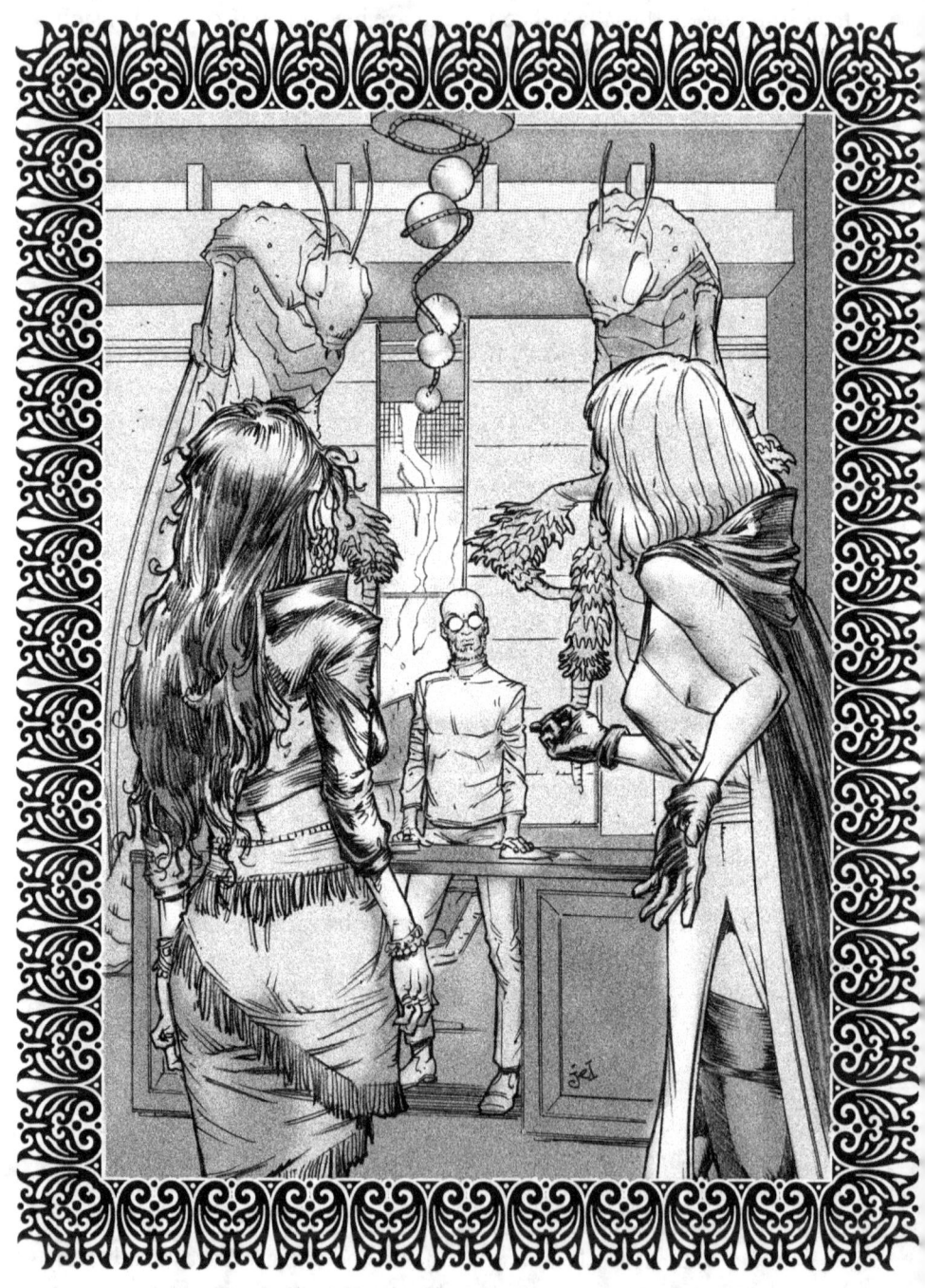

"That doesn't even come close to making sense!"

of different Counter-Earths that exist in universes parallel to ours. This alignment can have strange consequences as it affects the 'balance' of our Earth. Which brings us firstly to our subject in the main chamber."

By now, the slow-moving panes had finally terminated their course. Inside was a duplicate of the room above, minus the helicopters—in their stead was a large metallic dome. The giant insects were not threatening the pair, so Ellen stepped forward to examine this through the thick glass that separated the two rooms. With a sharp hiss, the dome began to retract.

There was a large shape inside, and it was moving with animal motion—muscles wobbled and rippled through gray flesh. Did they have an elephant trapped in there? It was tough to say, as the creature looked to be much larger than an elephant, both in terms of height and length. To say nothing of weight. Whatever was in there *felt* heavy, even from all this distance away. And it was obvious from the sounds it was making that it hated being penned up. Her eyes burned as she stared unblinking at the mass—and when the dome was fully down even the Domino Lady had to gasp.

The creature inside was, like the Insects of Zha-gai, not of this world. At least if it was, it was the product of the maddest of mad science. It looked to be rather like a titanic hippopotamus, but the head was nearly canine, at least around the eyes and teeth. It lacked a conventional snout, however, as its upper lip underwent a transformation, slowly transitioning from flesh to glinting metal. This metal formed a long, cruel blade which extended out from the creature's head. The length of the blade made the creature's gait topheavy—it almost looked like it was developed to walk upright, but was forced to resort to all fours due to the weight of the sword. Its wicked eye stared back at the Domino Lady, and for a second it appeared to make direct eye contact.

"What the hell is that thing?" Ellen blurted out.

"A Japanese member of my science division, Dr. Amamoto Hu, dubbed him 'Guiron,'" Norse explained. "The Insects of Zha-gai helped us extract him from Terra, one of the hypothetical Counter-Earths, with the use of their dimension-splitter. I knew we would need a powerful weapon if we were going to convince the world to understand our conception of the universe."

"You're going to unleash that creature on the world," Smarra said then—not as a question, but as a horrified statement of fact.

"Yes. You see, in order for us to get the world to devote its resources to reaching the Counter-Earth which we will transform in order to bring about change on this world, we must bring it to heel, first. Guiron will assist in that."

"Have I already said this doesn't make sense?" Ellen cut in then. "You're going to conquer the world...to take over another planet...which will then let you take over the world. Which you've already conquered!"

"The restless spirit of femininity which has corrupted this world is beyond even the masculine power of Guiron," Norse proclaimed. "We will need the energies of the Counter-Earth to fulfill our conquest. But in the meantime we can establish a minute extension of our dictatorship. It needn't be a large-scale conquest...just enough for us to establish a base which will suit our needs for reaching the Counter-Earth. Much of the technological provisions will be made by the Zha-gai Insects, but we will still need space, and privacy..."

"Space as in living space? You're no worse than that foaming would-be Napoleon out in Germany," said the Domino Lady.

"Even Hitler still allows himself association with women. Incidentally, ladies, your presence is beginning to put a foul taste on my tongue. I can't bear to be surrounded by inferior creatures. You've learned too much, which is admittedly my own fault, but I can't allow you to go on living. Even if I hadn't spoken a word to you, your sex is enough justification for me to kill you. There is no place for you in my utopia for men. Die knowing that your sacrifice makes the lives of good people better."

Both women had been assembling all the ideas he'd handed them into the greater mechanism—they tried to find logical in his mad ravings. It was halfway between metaphysical philosophy and the hard punch of sci-fi, and now, suddenly, tangible science fiction reached out and grabbed them as the Insects took them prisoner. With the adventurers hooked in their claws, they carried them on buzzing wings into the chamber of the monster called Guiron. They dropped them and returned back, and a touch of a button, Norse dropped a glass shield between himself and his two beautiful prisoners. Ellen's keen eyes spotted a microphone in his hand, and his voice continued over a loudspeaker:

"We've tested out Guiron's combat capabilities before, but we need to keep his bloodlust up if he's going to raid a city sometime soon. In any case, seeing people struggle against him is greatly amusing."

The Domino Lady stood up, as her legs had gone out from under her when the bug dropped her. She once more took up her gun in her hand, and she was fully prepared to shoot first and ask questions later. But the pistol clicked uselessly in her hand, its last shells expended. She ordinarily knew better that to overestimate such things.

She already knew that it was foolish to try to bring this thing down with bullets, though admittedly she was aiming for the sensitive-looking eyes. Near to those eyes, so intelligent and yet so brutish, were round hollows, echoes in the flesh, which rang with significance to her. At first, she did not overly menaced by the creature—its tremendous size likely counted against it in the speed department. And yet, now those disks cut into its skin were beginning to move, yielding to something that pushed its way through the skin. In these openings, now, were four-pointed stars, made of bone from the look of them. Ellen Patrick recognized these as duplicates of the ancient star-weapons of the ninjas.

But Smarra recognized them first. Her voice barked out the word, "Down!" but it was unnecessary. These enormous spiked crosses launched from the surface of Guiron's body, and flew at blinding speed towards the two women. Ellen's eyes were focused on evading the disks, but she couldn't help but glance at Smarra as she danced away. She was pretty agile herself, but Smarra made an art out of it. In a momentary half-thought pulse the Domino Lady felt her cheeks flush, and not from jealousy. When she landed, however, her face was as cool as usual when it came to having to deal with these sorts of challenges. Smarra, too, retained her calm.

The huge ninja-stars flew around them and boomeranged back towards Guiron. Smarra dashed her way back to Ellen, evading the returning projectile in the process, and her voice came over at a tone so repressed it almost scared the vigilante. "It's steering those *shuriken* with its mind. It's telekinetic. That, and that it can still *move* despite its bulk, proves that it comes from a place with different local physics."

"You say that pretty confidently. You must be a scientist of great merit," the Domino Lady shot back.

"I dabble," the Madonna replied. "I think that Norse was telling the truth. Those creatures back there have given him access to other dimensions. If that's true, it must also be true that he intends to...to change the nature of our cosmos somehow, change its balance, by anchoring our Earth to an interdimensional Earth of his creation..."

"Whether he's onto something or he's just a lunatic, we have to find that 'dimension-splitter' he mentioned and destroy it," the Domino Lady said. "After, of course—"

It was a good thing there was no need for further words, as Ellen's death would have been certain if she'd stayed still gabbing. She knew what was doing—she could handle herself. A backflip cleared her from the swing of Guiron's blade. The sword clattered hard against the chamber's metal floor, and she could see a score cut into it not a few inches deep. Where she landed was the platform used to carry up to where the choppers were waiting. The wave of relief she felt upon recognizing this elevator told her what to do next.

"Listen, Smarra, I don't think you have anything under those robes that can beat this thing. If we're going to kill it, we need to run away first."

"That's what I was thinking. I just need to get—ah!"

The Madonna's surprise seemed genuine—not often was she attacked by predators of Guiron's size. Despite his sluggishness, he always seemed to catch up to them with a burst of speed. One of his front paws, round and blunt at the bottom like a pachyderm, had caught onto her leg as it went out behind her. With a loud scrape he dragged her back across the ground, and Ellen thought she saw a trace of greedy slobber at his mouth as he drew his head back to decapitate her.

She sprinted forward then, leaving the sanctuary of the elevator platform behind. Throwing herself through the air she jabbed her leg out, and aimed at the very eye she'd wanted to shoot before. With a low groan of pain, Guiron reared back—her foot hadn't struck the eye, but she hit the soft flesh around it. It was enough to release Smarra, but as the creature pulled back he was also readying himself to bring his sword down again. Ellen unified her gesture of saving Smarra with that of saving herself. Running forward, she took up Smarra off the ground and dashed fast away from Guiron. He'd expected her to go dead away to the platform, instead of rescuing her companion. When they were back on the elevator, Smarra nearly struggled out of the Domino Lady's grip, her pride clearly hurt. At the same time, she respected one who saved her life.

"I owe you a favor," she said.

"No, you don't. You'd have done the same for me," Ellen said. She'd found the lever to move the lift, and she shoved it down comfortably now, knowing that despite his second and third winds, Guiron was still too lethargic to reach them in time. They watched as he bellowed below them, running his front legs against the edge of the lift shaft.

"Ellen Patrick, people have died *horribly* trying to earn my favor. You would be one of the biggest fools alive to refuse keeping it."

"Very well. I'm sure I'll think of something." The Domino Lady had other concerns. "Expect guys with guns at the top."

"Oh, I was counting on it. I may not have something hidden to stop

Guiron, but..." She reached into the folds of her crimson robe, and produced a hand grenade. "Nothing lethal—unfortunately. But I'd suggest shielding your eyes."

Eventually, the lift crossed the threshold, and it took only a moment's glance to confirm that the Domino Lady's prophecy came true. A second later, and it was like the sun was born again in this strange room below the sea. Half a dozen deep voices cried out in pain as their optic nerves were set alight. Even through her fingers and eyelids, Ellen could still see the blinding light.

When the manganese burst had subsided, Ellen swore that the Madonna hadn't shielded her eyes at all against that light. It didn't matter—though they had stopped the men with the big rifles, the time they'd bought meant they were far from the ground. Their only chance was in staying aboard until the mechanism completed its function. At the sounds of the elevator rising, the helicopters had taken off, as their pilots likely anticipated the arrival of their cargo. A plan began to hatch in the Domino Lady's mind, and she explained it hurriedly to the Madonna.

The elevator reached the top of the tower, and a peg emerged from one end of the platform that meshed with the tower. Then this peg thrust the platform forward. Far below them, but not too far, was the net. As Ellen stared down into through the holes in her mask, she turned once more to the Madonna, and asked, "Ever been part of a carnival act?"

The beautiful eyes flashed. "I think I'm going to find a liking for it," Smarra mused.

They dove.

Both of them knew the moves perfectly, as if they were practiced experts. Like two meteors they came down, and the coarse fiber of the net meshed around them as the fabric rippled upon impact. Clawing her way to air through the layers, Ellen began a desperate climb across the expanse of the net to where its edges were tied to the fleet of aircraft. Already, soldiers balanced on the rims of the helicopters aimed their guns at her, and at Smarra too once she worked her way free.

The Domino Lady was undeterred—no gun could scare her. She scrambled over the rim of the net at the point nearest to her, and took to crossing over to the helicopter by the long string of net that held it suspended. Not only was this her only way to proceed to the chopper, but if they wanted to blast her now they'd lose the net. A few bullets had whizzed by her, almost casual in their course, but her movement towards the shooters rippled out through the net, and made the choppers shake. The fliers weren't prepared for something like this to happen to them.

She reached up as soon as she was under the helicopter, and as the men above babbled among themselves to shoot her while she was below them she grabbed one of their ankles. She used this as leverage to haul herself up into where the action was—or where it would be. She brought it. So many times had her gorgeous shoulders captivated the eyes of admirers, but it was the arms that grew from them that counted. Really, it was the fists that counted most of all. Three soldiers and one pilot were all asleep and slung into the back. Hanging from the other helicopters were soldiers unsure of whether to fire on their fellow vehicle or not—they weren't even sure if they should fire at Smarra, now joining the Domino Lady. The vigilante laughed at their foolishness. She kept the bird level, but now that someone else was aboard to take over for her, she went out and cut the thread that connected the aircraft back to the net.

Up above them, the ceiling was beginning to open—it, too, was a hatch, and though there was only darkness above, it presumably opened up further into a secure location, one which would not bring in the sea. They could theoretically fly up and escape, but doubtlessly Norse could still find a way to transport Guiron out of here. And there was still the matter of the dimension-splitter. Whether it granted Norse access to another dimension or let him create his own—this was not power for man to wield. At once, Ellen told Smarra, "Go to the next level, and see if there's a place to land."

"Why?" Evidently the Madonna wished to go with the initial idea that appeared in Ellen's mind, getting away.

"Maybe there's something that can help us."

"A big 'maybe,' my dear."

"Do you also have a theory that the dimension-splitter is below the chamber Guiron's kept in?"

Smarra hesitated before answering, "There's no evidence of that."

"But you do think so."

"It seems architecturally fitting. And..."

"And you can feel something down there."

"...yes."

The Domino Lady didn't want to intrude further—for her own sake, rather than Smarra's. She could see now that Smarra was landing the helicopter on the floor that ringed the hatch, into which the doors of the hatch had retracted. There was just barely enough room to make it, and now, for the first time, the Domino Lady could hear the sounds of alarm klaxons warning that they were under attack. Dr. Norse, now far below them, was likely directing troopers to their location. While probably also working on freeing his living weapon.

As Ellen gazed down into the shaft, where the bulky, snarling shape of Guiron was still vaguely visible, Smarra tapped her shoulder, and pointed back towards a doorway they'd landed next to. Over the arch of this door read a plaque that said "Armory." Ellen's face lit up at that, and the two went forward with looting on their minds.

There was a pair of men inside, but in a fit of wishful thinking these men had hoped that the intruders were far away from them, not looming up in their faces. Ellen kicked one man's rifle away, while Smarra laid a punch into the other's stomach. They didn't take much more than that, and in a moment the ladies had their rifles. Smarra stared down at them and leveled the weapon at their fallen bodies, but the vigilante shoved it down and stared at her with a calm fury in her eyes. Smarra was not easily intimidated, and that did not change here, but she knew that there were more important things to be done. They quickly searched the long rows of shelves for the materials they needed, and confirmed that they had the proper provisions aboard the helicopter, as well. Ellen was shocked by the spread of weapons Norse had at his disposal. He could take over the White House and the Pentagon at once if he wanted to.

But they took only what they needed, from the broad assortment of grenades, rockets, pistols, and daggers. The plan was risky but they needed no reminder of that. The reminder came anyway, when the helicopter fleet from down below came up to follow the girls who'd stolen one of their brethren. The mercenaries aboard opened fire.

"Don't let them damage our bird! It's not yet time!" Smarra called. Ellen was aboard, and getting the rotors moving. These were some pretty advanced models that Norse was packing—they were fast, powerful, and could start up quickly. It wasn't long before they were the air, and like a rampaging bull they charged their attackers before bracing to drop.

This unexpected maneuver worked as imagined. The gunmen above them were at an awkward angle to shoot. They dropped down to where the net had been suspended—the Domino Lady scoped out the floor where the furious Guiron was patrolling. If he chose to strike at them, their chopper was wide open to his attack.

Attack he did. Once more his uncanny bone-*shuriken* emerged, and launched high into the air. Ellen let go of the controls, and as she backed away from them she saw that Smarra had already donned her parachute, and wielded her machine gun with some degree of pride. She had a cocky grin on her face as she watched Ellen pack her own 'chute over her long white dress.

They jumped at the same time Guiron's blades hit the rotors. Chopped them clean off—they didn't stand a chance. The shredded helicopter let out a scream even more horrible than Guiron's, and it rocked to one side like a ship bouncing off an iceberg; had they still been aboard, Smarra and Ellen would have been thrown off to break their necks down below. But they had double-checked that these 'chutes had been packed, and Smarra took pains to secure the sack they'd stolen from the armory. They'd pinched the machine guns but part of their scheme also involved stuffing that tied-down bag with as much dynamite and nitro as they could carry, with a few grenades to be on the safe side. The damage of the snapped blades echoed back into the rotor, and the device burst into a puff of shrapnel, turning fast into a clump of flames and escaping smoke.

They hoped the falling craft wouldn't miss its mark. Guiron was smart enough to evade, and they prayed for the luck to do the same. It wasn't Guiron they were trying to hit, anyway—but the ring which had once caged the giant monster was also the clasp that held that bottom hatch shut. The two women hit the ground and ran to the outer edge of the room.

The air screamed as the burning copter concluded its meteoric arc. The explosion nearly reached them, even at the edge of the chamber—Guiron screamed brutally and was thrown off his feet, smashing against the wall like a flipped turtle. Ellen observed over the shrieking heat that the blast-shield protecting Bluebeard Norse's office was no more, and if he and the Zha-gai Insects were still in there they were cooked alive. When at last the smog and flame cleared, she could see that the concussive force had blown the lock apart—though the doors hadn't moved far. It would still take some doing to get them far enough apart to squeeze through.

Both women knew this, and Smarra turned to look over the Domino Lady. Behind them, Guiron was climbing to his feet, already regaining his strength. "The feeling I'm getting is growing stronger. If I distract that thing, can you expose the splitter?"

"I can," the Domino Lady replied. "And then the only thing left to it is to blast it, I guess."

Smarra nodded, and the vigilante nodded back. Guiron roared, and raised his blade to brace for battle. Then Smarra's face broke out in a grin, and with a loud war-cry she charged off to clash with her giant foe.

As Ellen set to work on the barely-split doors covering Norse's alien device, she heard the blaze of machine gun fire as Smarra led her assault on Guiron. But the blasts of her gun soon had companions. Up above, the troops who'd staffed the helicopters were following the example the ladies had set and parachuted down to the floor. They were still too high up to aim accurately, and truth be told their nerves were rattled by all they'd witnessed in the last several minutes. Ellen pushed and shoved at the door, feeling it give and feeling gratitude for such, and allowed herself a brief smile, knowing that those men up there were likely also shaken by the rage of being outdone by people they so hated. They had armor and guns, and yet a nearly-unarmed blonde in a ravishing white evening dress was routing them.

She hoped that *schadenfreude* smile wouldn't be the last of her life. But the hatch-door was really moving now, and she could begin to see the outline of the dimension-device. Though she wasn't psychic or whatever it was that Smarra happened to be, she could sort of feel those strange vibrations now—like heat making the air shimmer, only cold. Or maybe it was better described as like a wind-tunnel, but with no push behind it. Even inactive, the device seemed *wrong*. She could see now it was a kind of cylinder, embedded in the floor and plugged into some incredible floor-wide power source (which she presumed extended down quite some distance); but even though she *knew* it was straight and rigid, rather like a pygmy farm silo, it didn't *look* that way to her. It squiggled somewhat—that was the first word she found that fit, "squiggled." It writhed, almost like a living thing, like a serpent. Its matter was blurred, stretched, and distorted, and it seemed to stem into too many angles of reality at once. Ellen couldn't entirely make sense of these thoughts as they entered her mind, just as she couldn't entirely make sense of the machine, but that stood up with what she knew about all of this so far. It wasn't quite yet safe to shoot but she was getting there...inch by inch.

Yet across the room, across the distortion field emitted by the dimension-splitter, a door opened. This door was just as far from Guiron and Smarra as it was from the Domino Lady, but now Smarra was being pushed back towards this door. Guiron was completely bulletproof, and she had been unable to strike at the softer tissues Ellen surveyed earlier. Coming through the door was Dr. Jilderay Norse, not dead as he had first appeared, and a platoon of Zha-gai Insects. As he approached, the troops above held their fire, but they had nearly landed. Upon the appearance of the Insects, Ellen's perception of the room became only more distorted—her sense of sickness intensified. But she gritted her teeth, even as she felt

"....she could feel...strange vibrations..."

the sweat pour down her forehead. She was stopping evil, just like her parents would have wanted, and as long as she remembered them there wasn't a chance of any of this stopping her.

She pointed the barrel of her gun square at the gibbering mass of shredded dimensions that was the Zha-gai splitter.

"No, Domino Lady!" roared Bluebeard Norse. "Don't do it! You don't what you'll—"

She squeezed the trigger. A hail of bullets flew fast into the distortion field, and the dense lead easily sliced through the alloys of the machine.

"—unleash—"

The cylinder exploded.

Ellen Patrick hadn't fully anticipated that that'd work. She nearly expected the bullets to have curved or something, and veered around the contraption she sought to blow away. But they had hit their mark, and the dimension-splitter was nothing but a funeral pyre to Norse's woman-hating plans.

Suddenly there was a black spot at the heart of the raging fire. It looked to Ellen at first to be a spot of smoke, but it didn't dissipate—it remained hovering within the heart of the inferno. And it was steadily growing, eating its way through the flame as if leeching its heat away. Now the edges of the fire were bending inward, confirming this theory. The light twisted and bent like a curtain being sucked into a vacuum cleaner, while the darkness grew and grew. And then the darkness broke. And there were *things* in the darkness.

Norse's voice, in the distance, in the wrong pitch: "You've cracked open a portal to the Multiverse—!"

Ellen was caught at the edge of the threshold, so she got a full glimpse of what awaited her within this gateway. And so much of it was just impressions. Thoughts, feelings, glimmers, whispers, brushing fingers in the shadows. Or what she thought were fingers. The first way of sensations that came off from this portal left her with the image of probing, wriggling arms, tentacles emerging from nowhere. At once, from scent (scent?) and intuition, the Domino Lady felt that these strange rubbery limbs were related somehow to the Insects which also walked with her into the flaw in space.

After that, she came across another layer—it was like she was from the outside rushing in, but the outside of what? Norse had mentioned a "Multiverse," but that was a new word to her. Did he mean multiple universes? She could see a vast cascade of moving disks now—perhaps those were planets, the myriad worlds of a thousand universes. It contradicted what she'd learned in church as a little girl, but so did a lot of things. By focusing, sometimes, she could bring herself close to these pulsating images of distant planets, and to her surprise she saw that a great many of them closely resembled the Earth. Boundless curiosity seized her, as she had to see what these other versions of the Earth looked like, even as she knew she had to pull back from the portal before she was consumed by it; but it was all like a dream, disappearing before she could remember, leaving behind meaningless words like "Sorcerer" and "Time King" and "Emperor." She was being pulled in deeper, to a version of her localized universe—she could see different dimensional versions of it, where things that weren't there were, and things that were there weren't. She had no idea that the universe looked like this. It was really more like several universes laid over each other, vibrating at different phantom rhythms, divided by faint pulses of song. Her universe was unique like that, in a way, or at least that was the impression she got. From a certain frame of reference she could see a version of her Earth where the noble were wicked and the evil just; she could see Earths where powerful weapons had turned the surface of the planet into nothing but a desert, inhabited by bizarrely-garbed lunatics or walking corpses. Sometimes flashes of colorful costumes similar to but more complicated than her own struck her eyes. For scattered moments the future, past, and present all became one in some sort of nauseating chronal slurry.

But she remained focused. And she began to see what Norse had once alluded to. Abstractions came so easily in the strange sight granted by this portal, and she began to see the outline of the scales that balanced her Earth. On the other platform was weighed a Counter-Earth. The mechanism that held them looked so tangible—it was a golden glimmer against diesel darkness. She didn't want to stare at it in case it was something holy. Instead, she turned her attention to the Counter-Earth, which was as inconstant as everything else within the gateway's limits. Over an expanse dotted by silver bats and silver men, and dancing starfish with cycloptic eyes in the center of their bodies, Ellen saw a dozen incarnations of the world that formed an invisible, intangible axis with the world she walked on (which she felt herself slipping from). As Terra, this planet had birthed Guiron, the only member of his species...perhaps he would return here again. He and his masters, the Insects and Dr. Norse alike, had been so much closer to the portal when it immanentized. They would be taken from this world.

Not her, though. The Domino Lady had been nearly drugged by the shock of gazing into the face of the Multiverse. Smarra, however, had witnessed such sights previously, and she removed Ellen from the portal before it was too late. The vigilante saw the world rippled before her, and reality reasserted itself—conventional reality, at least, for she knew at once that what she'd gazed upon had been real. For a moment there was a ringing in her ears and a whiteness which covered her vision, but it passed quickly. The portal collapsed, inhaling itself as it had drunk in the fire, and in its absence, Dr. Norse, the Insects of Zha-gai, and the monster Guiron were all vanished, along with a good portion of Norse's soldiers.

"A good portion." Smarra, setting Ellen on the ground, saw that there were some who still had some fight left in them. The Madonna took advantage of the Domino Lady's moment of weakness to unleash her rifle on the encroaching soldiers. She remembered the vigilante protesting her back up above, and she didn't want to take a chance of facing that resistance now. Yet she could only cut down half of Norse's remaining men before her rifle jammed. She swore an ancient curse under her breath.

There were three left, give or take a few—those extra few were cowering in some form, from all that had transpired. She considered sparing these few, but there was really no point. Those she disabled first—whether her blows to their necks induced death or unconsciousness she did not care. Ellen was still reeling behind her. Once the cowards were taken care of, Smarra moved in on the fighters. One by one, their puny skills crumpled before hers, no matter how loudly they roared, no matter how tough their stance or how big their muscles. Soon there was only one man left, and he had found his way to a dagger. He swung it without any degree of talent, powered only by sheer desperation.

"It doesn't matter what you've done here today! You've failed and we've triumphed!" Smarra laughed at his words, but he continued. "You've allowed Master Bluebeard to reach the Counter-Earth! The cosmic balance is his to control, as we always intended. Soon this world will be flooded with masculine energies, and—"

"I'm going to stop you there," the Madonna interrupted. "You are wrong. All of this has been wrong. There are forces unaccounted for in our philosophy and all that, true, but what I've done is nothing more than seal your leader, your monster, and much of your army in a parallel universe. Possibly several parallel universes if their luck is particularly bad. The Void had many deceptive images in it, and if you or Norse or anyone else saw a connection between 'Counter-Earth' and our world then it was merely an illusion."

The man seemed speechless—his dagger did not move outside of the nervous twitch running down through its blade. "I don't believe you."

"You do," she said, locking her eyes on his. "You do, I'm afraid. Whatever Bluebeard ends up doing on the world of his imprisonment, it won't be felt here. We are still in command of our destinies, same as always."

His face paled, and the hope drained from his eyes; it did so because he saw the truth in hers. This had all been her trap for "Master Bluebeard." Everything that had occurred this day had been for the purpose of sealing him beyond this universe, forever.

And he was the one who would carry the lesson he'd learned to the outside world. If he was very, very lucky. Her plan wasn't quite finished yet. For now, she laid a sock into his face, and he would be out for quite a few minutes.

One of the pilots had taken pains to land a copter up on the floor up above. Smarra made a break for the hatch, counting on Ellen to rise quickly and follow her. She counted correctly. The Domino Lady stirred, the images of the Multiverse slowly becoming normalized within her psyche. She wiped her long strands of blonde hair from her face, checking to make sure her mask was still mounted properly. Thus satisfied, she started running, having also spotted the chopper up above.

Upon spotting the Madonna's robed form, she called out, "Smarra!"

Smarra turned. "We have to destroy this place. If we don't, someone will find it, and figure out how to build another dimension-splitter."

"You're right. There's no other way."

And Ellen could see now that the helicopter they planned to take was different from the others. Attached to its base were long tubes which ended in wicked-looking spikes. The Domino Lady recognized these, and knew at once what they had to do with them.

Far above them, the last of the enormous hatches had finished opening, exposing the bright shine of daylight. Dimly, the pair could make out flocks of ocean gulls circling above them. They would soon join those gulls in the air above the Californian Pacific. Nearby, the people of Los Angeles were likely going on about their business as usual; unaware of what was happening under the ground. Ellen wondered how many men in that city would have sided with Norse if he had brought Guiron up to obtain space for his laboratory. She thought of all of the women she had hopefully saved.

They climbed into the helicopter, and took off, once they reached the proper floor. Below them crackled the remnant flames of the shattered wreck of the Zha-gai device. On the exposed floors there were still yet further masses of soldiers appearing, who fired potshots at them. Ellen was flying, so Smarra opened fire on them with her rifle. She was very nearly out of ammo from her prolonged duel with Guiron, but she was just trying to spook the already-frightened combatants. Floor after floor they left behind, until finally, they were at the lip of the exit out. Ellen knew what she had to do—the missiles strapped to the chopper's undercarriage were long since armed. As they gained altitude, she let them loose.

There was a deafening blast, like a wrecking ball smashing down a skyscraper. The spike of heat and flame upwards carried their bird away from the cone—a quick glance to the side on Smarra's behalf revealed that the landing gear had melted, with the escaping slag hissing against the surface of the cold blue water. But they'd escaped the bulk of the blast and rocked only slightly. The facility they'd left down below was not so lucky.

As they'd hoped, the rocket had punched a hole in the retaining wall of the shaft. The ocean was starting to pour in, and wherever the metal and concrete had splintered, there were soon long wounds slicing downward, tearing apart the whole beast segment by segment. The ocean covered nearly all of the Earth, and there was no resisting its terrific force.

Soon the base was beyond visibility, as its upper limits were crushed by the great fist of water squeezing about it. The rain of liquid and metal would have smashed whatever little survived of the dimension-device to tiny fragments. A whirlpool swirled downward like the mouth of Charybdis, and the Domino Lady let free a sigh of relief.

What a terrible mess it had all been. Guilt washed over her as she realized all her attempts to preserve life on this case had been for nothing. Not unless there were ways out of the facility that Norse's team knew about, which remained secret to her. In the end, however, the vast majority of the men in service to the Madonna's counterpart were dead, and the man himself was now far away from here. They had brought about peace and stopped an enormous beast from destroying the city. It was time to rest.

She put them down on the beach, letting the soft sand accommodate the burns on the ship's bottom. It was still too early for the beach to be populated, though some folks were coming down now to examine the source of the blast they'd heard. Silently, the two made their way out of the helicopter and down the length of the beach, and Ellen thought it was a little funny that no one seemed to notice them, despite their costumes. She knew from experience that much of the world of stealth was banking on ordinary folk always facing the wrong way when it came to important things.

Once they were away from everyone else—finding themselves a beachhead hill, masked under the shadow of a tree and the height of the hardy grass—Smarra began to laugh. "Thank you, sister. You've brought me much entertainment tonight, and you've helped me deal with a tremendous threat to our Order and all we protect. Please, won't you reconsider my offer?"

"To join you? No, I'm sorry. I've got to swing solo."

"Oh? Well, team-ups like this must be rather rare for you."

"They are."

"Won't you enjoy this one a little while longer?"

Smarra pulled close to the Domino Lady, her eyes shimmering, her hands looped tight around the dress-clad form. The fabric was so soft—the skin under, so much softer.

Ellen grinned widely and returned the embrace. "I guess I've got a little extra time."

And they laid down on the hill, obscured now completely by the tall spires of grass.

On the dusty surface of Counter-Earth, Dr. Jilderay Norse regarded his prospects.

The Insects of Zha-gai were, in their infinite wisdom, quite understanding. They had used their technological miracles to make reasonable forms of shelter for him and his men, though they didn't need shelter themselves, and they had been quite open to proceeding with the plan. There were lifeforms here which they could go to work on, and before the end of the doctor's lifespan, they could perhaps turn these primitive mammals into beings capable of interbreeding with humans. The descendants of his militia group would populate this nameless world, and if he worked hard, he would ensure that the society that thrived here would hold onto his ideals. Though he hadn't heard what the Madonna had said to his soldier, he knew, somehow, by the merit of voyaging through the interuniversal void, that this world had no "energetic" impact on his native Earth. There were too many Counter-Earths out there in the void, in simultaneous existence and nonexistence. Maybe his world would make a difference on Earth, but now he knew only doubt.

They were lost in time as well as space. He didn't know how he understood that, but he suspected that in some relative way, it was now a very ancient time back in his native continuum. He would not yet be born for millennia—and yet here he was. Almost funny, in its own way.

He shuddered, thinking of the future that the philosopher-kings had planned for this world. It was great to consider a world where men had finally regained control over women, but at the same time, he had not anticipated his descendants to be non-human. He hoped that the Insects would provide them with attractive brides. To come all this way only to be forced into a loveless marriage with something *ugly* would be the ultimate insult—the ultimate sign that the Multiverse was bent against men. Old voices came back to him as he mulled over these thoughts, calling him crazy for thinking such things. But he wasn't crazy. He knew he wasn't.

He thought of insults and in turn he thought of the Order of the Madonna. They always claimed to bring "safety" to women, as if the world didn't already coddle and shelter them in every way imaginable. They were just a pack of elitist man-haters. It was his right to beat his wife; to use her in any way he saw fit. For those girls to bust in and take that from him was morally wrong.

He would grit his teeth and ride this out, like a real man. Already he knew he needed a symbol to rally his men around before they lost their sanity. He knew already what it would be. Though they had been separated from him, they had all looked to Guiron, in their days on Earth, as a beacon of hope for the change yet to come. They didn't know where or when he was now, but perhaps they could recall his image, and they would have something to worship—something to draw upon to call up a name for their newfound home, a name to respect. His great masculine blade would remind them of why they were here; remind them through its great power to Stab, to Pierce.

To Gore.

And while Dr. Norse planned the name of his new planet, the Insects of Zha-gai prayed in silence. It was a prayer of gratitude, offered to their ancient god, for the success they presently enjoyed. Indeed, there would much chaos on this world, for it would be born in blood and hedonistic cruelty. All had followed the shapeless pattern, the unspeakable plan woven by the mad ravings of the Great God Azathoth.

The End

INSPIRATIONS

I wrote "Unbalanced" a short time after the release of my double-story book *Deus Mega Therion / The Divine Mrs. E*, which was published in July 2017 by Odd Tales Productions. It was around the time that book came out I noticed Airship 27 had a Domino Lady collection that was looking for stories. I'd been interested in writing a Domino Lady tale ever since finding out about her, but I also saw the story as an opportunity to wrap up some loose ends I'd been meaning to touch on in *The Divine Mrs. E* but couldn't incorporate properly. That story, along with *Deus Mega Therion* and their mutual follow-up *Kinyonga Tales* (also from Odd Tales Productions, February 2018), are massive crossover stories, tying together a number of ideas and theses for crossovers which I've had for quite some time, involving stories from fiction's beginning to its present. (Some of these ideas I still explore in my stories of superhero Bloody Mary and a series of crossover tales I've posted on Archive of Our Own under the name "AdamMudman.") One of the central premises of *The Divine Mrs. E* is that it centers around an organization made up of nearly every fictional women-only gang, cult, and alien race united into a common history, based around helping women and improving their social standing. This organization is, as those of you who have read "Unbalanced" may have guessed, the Order of the Madonna—a group initially inspired in part by the Order run by Sax Rohmer's Sumuru, whom Smarra is meant to be. Since the Domino Lady is essentially *the* foremost lady hero of the pulp era I could think of no one better to follow as I explored what the Order was up to decades before the events of *The Divine Mrs. E*.

Through "Unbalanced" I was able to hint at some of the other members or potential members of the Order who didn't show up in my book—fans of John Updike and Jesus Franco, for example, may find some interesting nods. However, I also wanted to talk about fiction that represents the opposite of the Order of the Madonna, and their goals of helping women, so I looked to particularly misogynist stories to draw from when imagining this story's villains. "Christian, Lord Kelso" is one example of this sexist fiction, if the riddle of his identity can be decoded by the reader. I realized then that a story tying the Order in with the creation of a certain fictional planet renowned for its misogynistic society—the identity of which, again, can be decoded from the story—allowed for the possibility of exploring the various fictional versions of the "Counter-Earth" theory as well. Once I remembered that the titular monster from *Gamera vs. Guiron*, the greatest of the original *Gamera* films, was from a version of Counter-Earth, I had all my pieces, and it was just a matter of putting them together. I'm fairly pleased with my ability to present these theoretical/academic elements while balancing them with the kind of action pulp fans have come to expect.

Adam Mudman Bezecny started writing nine years after the 1994 lab accident that created him. Seven years later he adopted the name and infinite creed of "Mudman." Since then he's summarily failed several destinies in White Bear Lake, Minnesota, and Morris, Minnesota. He's also experimented lovingly with filmmaking and film criticism. He first came in contact with the pulp world when Alan Moore and Kevin O'Neill's *The League of Extraordinary Gentlemen* introduced him in turn to the works of Philip Jose Farmer and the Wold Newton Universe. (A pulp-themed short story of his, "Revelation of the Yeti," will be featured in Black Coat Press's *Tales of the Shadowmen Volume 12*, featuring Doctor Omega, Ki-Gor, and Nora the Ape-Woman.) His true passion in writing, however, is telling stories of a Multiverse he's been creating for his entire life. Two stories of his Multiverse, the sci-fi/horror/fantasy/pronominal-nightmare piece *Dieselworld* and the blog-based horror invasion yarn *Words from the Inner Circle*, can be found at (http://dieselcascade.blogspot.com/2013/07/1.html) and (http://innercirclechats.blogspot.com/2014/05/introduction.html), respectively. A Multiverse novel exposing the true stories behind the filmography of independent underground Earth-20181 moviemaker Herald deKööl is in the works.

OVER A BARREL

By Gene Moyers

*E*llen Patrick sipped from a glass of water while vaguely wishing it was something stronger. Unfortunately, Marconi's was one of Oakland's nicer restaurants; too nice to serve bootleg alcohol. She smiled and shook her full head of long blonde hair; at least she could still smoke. She lit up a cigarette and glanced at her watch. Barbara was late.

Ellen Patrick was well known in southern California social circles. With her tall good looks and winning personality she was welcome at any party, movie premiere or Hollywood gathering. She moved in several social circles and knew many rich or influential people across the Southland. This served her well when she assumed her alternate personality of the mysterious Domino Lady.

Right now though, Ellen was on vacation. She had come north to spend some time with her good friend Roger McKane. They had had a wonderful time in San Francisco doing the town but their time was coming to an end. On her last day in town Ellen had called her old school friend Barbara Girardi and made a luncheon date.

As Ellen mused, Barbara Girardi made her appearance. She was a looker, with long dark brown hair and a tan that showed she had earned her figure with lots of outside exercise. The two girls greeted each other excitedly with a hug. They then spent a leisurely lunch going over old times. Barb's family lived in Napa and had been growing wine there for nearly fifty years. Prohibition had brought tough times to the Girardis and the wine industry generally. Ellen was interested in how they managed to keep their winery afloat. Barb smiled as she glanced at her watch, "That's why I had you meet me here. In a few minutes I'm meeting Monsignor Conroy at St. Teresa's to talk about additional orders of sacramental wine."

Ellen showed her surprise, "You're making sacramental wine?"

Her brunette friend nodded her head, "Absolutely. It's one of the things keeping us in business. A few of the wineries around Napa have made deals with various dioceses to make sacramental wine."

"I had no idea that was still legal"

"Oh yes! There are several loopholes in the *Volstead Act* that allow us to operate in a limited way."

Ellen shook her head, "I'd like to hear more about that. If there are any

44

alcohol related loopholes to be found I know some people down south that would love to hear about them."

Barb laughed as she reached for her purse, "I'll be glad to help but now I've got to get down to St. Teresa's."

The two young women paid their bill and exited the restaurant. Ellen said, "Let's take my car." Her friend agreed and they hopped into Ellen's roadster and were quickly on their way. It was only a few blocks and within two minutes the huge gray, stone building was in sight. Ellen frowned as they slowed, "Uh oh, what's that?"

She pulled the roadster to a stop behind a police car parked at the curb. On the sidewalk a uniformed officer was talking to two men dressed in overalls and work shirts. A priest in black cassock stood by looking anxious. The open car had barely stopped rolling before Barb was out of it and trotting toward the group of men. As she reached them, the priest turned to her with a sad look on his face. Barb queried, "Father, what's going on?" She turned to the other three men, "Sam? Tony? What's happened?"

The policeman spoke up, "I'm afraid there's been a robbery, miss. Are you involved in all this?" Before Barb could answer one of the workmen spoke, "I'm sorry, Miss Girardi. They had guns. We couldn't do anything. Before we knew it they had the truck and left us standing there in the street." There was a bit of confusion as everyone tried to talk at once. Soon though everyone settled down and the story was told.

Sam and Tony were long time Girardi employees. They had been driving a truck loaded with sacramental wine to St. Teresa's. Barb was to meet them there to discuss the diocese's next purchase. Two blocks from the cathedral, a man had staggered out into the street in front of the truck and fallen. The drivers had screeched to a stop and got out to help. Suddenly another man on the sidewalk had produced a gun, as had the supposedly injured man. At gun point they took the truck and disappeared into traffic. The drivers ran to the Cathedral, alerted the priest and called police. The responding officer was just taking their statements when Ellen and Barb had pulled up.

Eventually a police detective arrived to open an investigation. With Barb's statement given, Ellen volunteered to drive her back to her car. Once in the roadster Ellen turned to her friend, "This is bad isn't it?"

Barb replied sadly, "This hi-jacking is going to set us back something awful. Not to mention it leaves the Church in the lurch as well."

Ellen was thoughtful for a moment, "You realize this was planned. They knew exactly when you were to deliver the wine."

Barb frowned, "You mean we were targeted?"

"It sure sounds like it."

"But why?"

"Does your father have anyone who would like to see him ruined? An old enemy perhaps?"

"No. No one would want to hurt dad."

"Well someone certainly went to a lot of trouble to hurt your family or... perhaps your winery," Ellen said significantly.

Barb responded sourly, "Same difference. You hurt the winery and you hurt my family. Now I've got to go home and tell Dad."

Ellen volunteered, "I don't have to head home tomorrow. I could stay around for a couple of more days. Maybe something will turn up. I've got a friend who knows a lot of local cops."

Barb brightened immediately, "That would be great. You could come out to Napa and stay with us." They quickly made plans before parting at Barb's car. Ellen then turned her car toward the ferry.

She reached the terminal just as a ferry was about to sail. As she stood by the rail watching the San Francisco skyline ahead Ellen thought about the new bridge to Oakland they would begin building next year. They were also planning a bridge from San Francisco across to Marin County. The new bridges would make trips across the bay a lot easier but she would miss the ferry trips. The views of the city and the Golden Gate were breath taking.

Quickly they neared the Ferry Building. The huge building on the Bay with its four sided clock tower was located where Market Street met The Embarcadero. A San Francisco landmark, it had withstood the 1906 earthquake and was still the main connecting point with other cities on the Bay. Soon she was driving off the ferry and headed uptown.

Back at her suite at the *Mark Hopkins* Ellen dialed a local number. When a receptionist answered she asked for Roger McKane. There was a pause before a confident young voice came on the line, "Hello, Roger McKane."

"My, aren't we formal?"

"Ellen? I thought you'd be headed home by now."

Ellen leaned back on the luxurious sofa and laughed softly as she puffed her cigarette, "You're not trying to rush me out of town are you, Roge?"

"You know better than that Ellen. I don't see enough of you as things are. But you said you were leaving after lunch with your friend. By the way, how did that go?"

"Okay…as far as it went. Actually, I'm going up to stay with Barb in Napa for a couple of days before heading back south."

"Uh, that's nice," Roge sounded a bit surprised.

"Uh huh, and since I don't know much about Napa I thought I'd call and see what you could tell me."

McKane was suspicious now, "You mean about the best restaurants?"

"Actually like what's going on up there in law enforcement circles, crime and what not."

There was a pause, "Uh huh, and just what kind of trouble are you getting into now?"

Ellen smiled as she answered in her most innocent voice, "I'm just going up there to visit Barb…and maybe give her a hand with a little problem."

Ellen heard the smack of flesh against flesh and had no trouble imagining Roge smacking his palm against his forehead, "I remember the last time you 'just helped a friend out.' Didn't it end up with the coast guard involved and us abandoning ship?"

Suppressing a laugh, Ellen replied casually, "This is nothing like that. I just want to know what the political climate is like around Napa. Barb's family is in the wine business and she's a little concerned with local law enforcement."

Reluctantly Roge replied, "Well, if that's all, I suppose I could ask around a little. Are you still at the *Mark*?" Ellen replied affirmatively and Roge promised to get back to her before the end of the day.

Roge was as good as his word. It was nearly five o'clock when Ellen answered her ringing phone to find the young detective on the line.

"Oh Roge, I hope you've got all the dirt on Napa for me."

He gave a short bark of laughter before replying, "Well, I don't know if I've got it all but there's plenty of dirt to go around."

Ellen grimaced, "I was afraid of that."

"As you would expect, any area that depends on the alcohol industry was hit hard by prohibition. A lot of wineries went bankrupt. Some plowed their grapes under and planted other crops. A few started making grape juice but I hear that wine grapes aren't best for that. A few have managed to stay in business on the fringes by cutting deals with various dioceses to make sacramental wine…" Ellen cut in, "That's what Barb's family does."

There was a pause before Roge asked, "Are they the ones that got hijacked today?"

Realizing she was going to get another worried lecture Ellen replied in a light tone, "Actually, yes. She's really upset and I am going up to Napa for a couple of days to stay with her."

"Uh huh, you're not going to do any snooping around up there. Are you?"

"C'mon Roge, I'm just going up to keep Barb company. The only reason I asked you to check into things was so I could get the lay of the land."

A pause, "Riiiight. Anyway times are tough for a lot of the wineries. There's even one that's selling "bricks" of dehydrated grape juice…complete with directions on how not to make wine with it." Ellen laughed briefly as he continued, "There's a lot of bootlegging going on up there, mainly sold to local restaurants and private clubs. The word is that there aren't a lot of organized gangs involved like back east. It's mainly locals trying to make dollar on the side. Don't stray off the road very far or you'll trip over a secret still or a Federal agent searching for it."

"What about on the other side of the law?"

"Well, as you can imagine where there's money; there's corruption. In fact the former District Attorney, some guy named Rawles was forced to resign a few months ago due to charges of corruption."

Ellen said thoughtfully, "Really? That is interesting."

"Yeah, but that's not the worst of it. The Feds are snooping all around and paying good money for tips, I hear. I'm surprised there are any wineries left in business at all."

Ellen's mind raced. It seemed like Napa was going to be a complicated place. She told her friend, "Thanks Roge, you've been a dear for helping out."

He dropped his voice a level, "There's more. Mostly details, I could come over later and we could discuss it more."

"Well, I do have to get packed and bathed if I'm checking out early tomorrow…"

"Then you'll need someone to scrub your back, won't you?"

Ellen's voice dropped to a husky tone, "I suppose I could use a little help…"

"About seven?"

"I'll be here."

Late the next morning Ellen drove her roadster off the Ferry into Richmond, across the bay from San Francisco. She was caught in a bit of city traffic but soon made it through town and drove north along the Lincoln Highway. She crossed new Carquinez Bridge and reached Vallejo by eleven o'clock. There she took state Highway 29 north and finally reached Napa about noon.

Napa was a sleepy little town of several thousand people. Ellen did not stop there but continued up the highway for several more miles until she found the road leading to the Girardi property and turned off the highway. A tree lined drive led to a group of well-kept buildings. As she pulled the roadster to a stop in front of the large Victorian style house Barb appeared, waved and ran down to meet her, "Oh, Ellen I'm so glad you're here!"

"Me too!" She looked around, "Things haven't changed a bit."

"Why should it? My grandfather built things to last. The house is nearly fifty years old."

The two girls hugged and Barb led her around the house toward a large brick building. Two men were standing in front of it.

Barb waved and said to Ellen, "There's dad, with Mr. Beringer. He has a sacramental wine contract for another diocese." After being introduced to the wine growers, Barb and Ellen spent the rest of the afternoon visiting. Barb gave her details of how the local wineries were doing. She also told Ellen about a couple of wineries that had recently gone bankrupt.

Barb was mildly surprised when Ellen explained something had come up requiring her to return to San Francisco and sadly had to change her plans about staying with them. Ellen had decided to drive back to Napa. She felt bad about letting Barb down, but should she attract any undue attention she didn't want it to be connected to the Girardis. She reached Napa late in the afternoon and drove straight to the county courthouse.

Inside at the county clerk's office they were very helpful. Checking the records she found that the two wineries that Barb had told her about were still listed under the original owners. Thinking this somewhat strange she borrowed a telephone book from the clerk and quickly located two real estate agents nearby. It was late afternoon but both were in walking distance from the courthouse so she decided to pay them a visit.

She pushed through the door of the first office and was greeted by a woman behind a desk, "Hello, may I help you?"

Ellen gave her a smile, "Yes, I hope so. I'd like to speak with someone about possibly buying some property."

The woman smiled back and moved toward an inner office, "Well, if you'll wait here a moment I'll get Mr. Dunbarton."

A moment later she was back followed by a plump, prosperous looking man in a suit. He held out a hand, "I'm Horace Dunbarton. Can we be of service, Miss uh ...?"

Ellen held out her hand in return, "My name is Page, and I hope so." Dunbarton quickly ushered Ellen into his inner office and offered her a chair. Seated at his desk he folded his hands and asked, "What can I do for you today?"

"Well Mr. Dunbarton, I'm up here looking around for property. My family is located in southern California but my father wants to invest in farmland in this area. He asked me to come up and look around. If anything looks promising, he may want to put in a bid."

Dunbarton looked a little surprised but recovered quickly, "May I say that your father is very discerning. It is fine farm country hereabouts, and prices are somewhat depressed. But I am surprised that your father sent such a young, uh..."

"Woman?" Ellen favored him with a thin smile, "My father would be very disappointed if I couldn't put my business degree from Berkeley to use."

Dunbarton colored slightly, "I didn't mean to offend Miss Page. How much land were you looking for?"

"Several hundred acres; I understand several former wine properties have come on the market recently."

"Well, many wineries have sold out over the years due to Prohibition or have converted their vines to other crops."

"And have there been any selling recently?"

The real estate agent hesitated then said, "There was a recent sale that we brokered."

Ellen nodded, "Good. Do you have any other former wine properties available?"

There was a definite hesitation now, "Uh no, unfortunately."

Ellen frowned, "That's too bad. May I ask how much the previous property went for?"

Dunbarton blustered a bit, "Well uh, of course all of our transactions are confidential. But I can say that the price was quite reasonable for this area."

Ellen stood up, "Then I'm sorry to have troubled you Mr. Dunbarton." He stood up also, anxious to make amends, "If any other former wine properties come on the market, would you still be interested Miss Page?"

"Of course."

"Then perhaps if you would leave an address where you can be reached…"

Ellen nodded and quickly gave the real estate agent a bogus address and phone number in Santa Barbara. Then thanking him, she left. The second real estate agent was less helpful. He claimed to not have handled any wine properties recently. He confirmed Dunbarton's view that property prices were depressed.

By now it was nearly five o'clock and Ellen was ravenous. She found a small hotel in the downtown area and checked in. She ate dinner in a diner near her hotel and returned to her room early. She lay down on the bed in her clothes and was quickly asleep.

Ellen awoke up just after midnight. Quickly undressing, she changed into a long white dress. From her purse she took a small automatic pistol and slipped it into a holster high up on her thigh under her dress. On the other thigh she positioned a capped syringe. She then swung a long black cloak around her shoulders, fixed it at her throat and finally positioned a black mask over her eyes. The mysterious Domino Lady now stood in Ellen Patrick's room.

Checking that the hallway was empty, the masked woman stepped out and walked quickly to a window at the end of the hall that looked out over the alley. It was quiet and appeared deserted. She raised the sash, ducked forward and swung one leg over the sill to rest on the metal fire escape. She climbed through and softly lowered the sash behind her. Moments later she was dropping off the ladder into the alley.

She followed the light at the end of the alley to a quiet side street. Her roadster was parked just down the street and in seconds she was behind the wheel. With the top up it was unlikely that anyone could see her masked visage but she still drove carefully through the quiet town. Napa was a small farm town and the masked woman saw no one on the street as she drove toward the real estate office she had visited earlier. She parked around the corner from it and slipped quietly along the street to the office door.

Keeping her head turned toward the street to watch for approaching cars, she worked her lock pick by feel. Two minutes of work and the lock clicked open and she slipped inside. Using a small pocket flashlight taken from a concealed pocket in her cloak the Domino Lady moved to a set of file cabinets and began searching them. She shielded her light carefully to keep it from being seen by anyone passing by the street windows.

It didn't take long to find the file she was looking for. Sure enough the winery was listed as being sold, and at quite a reasonable price, Ellen thought. Interestingly the sales date was listed as over a month ago. Why hadn't the sale been recorded with the county? Most interesting the purchaser was listed as one Ralph J. Rawles. This caught the Domino Lady's attention. Could this be the same Rawles that Roge had mentioned?

Quickly replacing the file she searched for the other winery that Barb had told her about. It too was here. This sale was listed as several months ago but it too had not been recorded with the county. The purchaser again was Ralph Rawles. The Domino Lady replaced this file as well and stood thoughtfully in the dark. If the Rawles who was buying up bankrupt wineries was the same ex-DA Roge had told her about it would explain why he was forced from office. She decided that he would bear a closer look.

She glided her way to the front door and was just about to open it when headlights appeared to her left. Ducking down the Domino Lady watched as a local police car drove slowly past on the deserted street. When it had passed out of sight she slipped out the door, turned and relocked it. She walked quickly around the corner to her car. Once inside she drove back to her hotel and re-entered her room via the alley and fire escape. Minutes later she was in bed and asleep.

The next morning Ellen pulled her car up in front of a modest rented house on a quiet side street in Napa. A quick call to Barb after breakfast had established that the former owners of Markham Winery were living in town at this address.

Ellen walked to the porch and knocked on the door. It was opened by a middle aged, gray haired, rather stooped man, "Yes?"

"Mr. Markham? My name is Ellen. Barb Girardi gave me your address. I'd like to speak with you if I may."

Markham hesitated for a moment before swinging the door wide, "Please come in."

Ellen entered the small, tidy living room and accepted a seat on the sofa. The former wine maker offered her some lemonade. Ellen declined and Markham asked, "Why would Barbara Girardi send you here?"

"Well sir, I know it's a sore subject but I need to ask you a few questions about your winery." She held up a hand, "I wouldn't ask if it wasn't important. The Girardis are worried that something bad may happen to them just as it happened to you."

Markham stared hard at Ellen for a moment than seem to relax, "Very well. The Girardis are good people. Ask your questions."

"Can you tell me how you lost your winery?"

The old man closed his eyes and shook his head, "It was the government. I had to sell out. It was the only way to pay the fines."

Ellen frowned, "Maybe you should start at the beginning."

Taking a deep breath Markham nodded and started in, "Do you know that under the Volstead Act it isn't a crime to own or drink alcohol? It's only illegal to manufacture, sell, transport or import alcohol. In fact each family is allowed to make up to two hundred gallons of 'intoxicating beverages' for home use per year." He paused and gave her a small smile, "Now that's actually a lot of alcohol and some families might be tempted to sell some on the side. To stop that from happening Federal agents came and inventoried our 'family wine' regularly. They even counted the empty bottles. We played it honest and didn't sell any of our private wine.

"But one night the old wine cellar was robbed. They took hundreds of bottles. We reported it to the sheriff and thought that we'd done the right thing. Then two weeks later Federal agents showed up at the winery and raided us. They claimed our private wine had been found during raids on restaurants and speakeasies. I was arrested and prosecuted.

"In the end I was fined over five thousand dollars. I couldn't pay the fine or my lawyer's fees so I was forced to sell the winery." He looked down at his feet and said sadly, "We didn't get what the land was worth but it was enough to pay off my debts."

Ellen was silent for a moment as she pondered this sad story. Finally she spoke softly, "Do you know who the buyer was?"

Markham shook his head, "It was handled by a local real estate agent. He said the buyer was from out of town." Ellen said nothing at this but inside she could feel her temperature rising. So that was it. Rawles and some confederates had robbed the Markhams, spread some of their wine around and tipped off the Feds. Then he sat back and let the law do his work for him. When the dust settled he bought the Markham's vineyards at a bargain rate. He had no doubt paid Dunbarton to keep the sale quiet and probably someone in the sheriff's office as well to "lose" Markham's robbery report. She frowned; it was a neat scheme.

Aloud she said, "I'm sorry for you, Mr. Markham. You've been wronged. If it's any solace, I'm going to see if I can keep this from happening to the Girardis." She stood up, "I'm going to speak with them now." She traded a few peasantries with Markham and said goodbye. Back in her roadster she

"Do you know who the buyer was?"

decided that her next move would be to find Rawles. Driving downtown she located a phone booth in a drug store and called Barb. She advised them to keep close watch on their family wine stock and to beware of any strangers looking around their place. She then looked up Rawles in the phone book. There was only one entry and she decided to drive over to it.

Rawles' house was a nice but not overly large home on a quiet Napa street. As she drove slowly past it, Ellen saw a man come out of the front door, lock it and walk to a car in the driveway. Ellen drove a block ahead and pulled over to the curb. She ducked down and peeked over the seat back. Rawles pulled out onto the street turned the other way and drove off. Ellen quickly sat up, turned her car around in a driveway and followed the ex-DA.

Five minutes later he entered a restaurant on a downtown street. Glancing at her watch she decided with a smile that it was time for lunch. Parking nearby she made her way to the Italian restaurant. Inside she was shown to a booth along one wall. Water was brought, as was a menu. As Ellen pretended to study it she saw Rawles at a table near the back. He seemed to be waiting for someone.

She ordered lunch and settled in to wait. As the waiter brought her lunch a few minutes later, a large man in a rumpled suit entered the restaurant and headed for Rawles' table. As he passed Ellen got a glimpse of a revolver holstered on the big man's hip.

The food was good and Ellen took her time, enjoying her meal and looking casual. She tried to listen in on Rawles' conversation with the big man. Unfortunately they were too far away for their low voices to carry. Finally Ellen stood up and made her way past their table to the rest room. Minutes later she passed by again and heard Rawles say, "Not tonight, tomorrow at nine. Bring the truck." She then made her way to the front of the restaurant. There she paid her bill and asked the plump, smiling woman at the cash register, "Who's that big man at the back table?"

The woman seemed surprised, "With Mr. Rawles? Why that's the sheriff, of course." She looked at Ellen curiously. Ellen smiled and said, "I'm from out of town." Exiting she found her car and drove away.

Earlier Ellen had gotten directions from Barb and now she drove north out of town searching for the two bankrupt wineries. It took a bit of doing but Ellen finally located the first winery. There she found the homestead, winery building and all out buildings apparently abandoned and surrounded by uncut grass with no sign of occupancy for months.

Back in her car Ellen continued searching. A half hour later she found the entrance to the former *Markham Winery*. A long tree lined, gravel driveway led to the empty homestead. The two story house was clearly unoccupied. There were some new *No Trespassing* signs posted but no other sign of recent habitation. Behind the house and large storage barn, the winery itself had been built into the low hillside. There was a business entrance with boarded over windows and twenty yards to the right was a large set of wooden double doors closing off a large entrance into the hillside.

Examination showed the small door was locked. The lock looked to Ellen as if it hadn't been opened in months. The large double doors were another matter. The padlock that secured them was obviously new and shiny. Correctly deciding that the new lock would be much easier to open Ellen went to work on it with her lock picks. Within three minutes the lock popped open and she swung one door wide to let in some daylight. Inside was a loading area. There were wooden pallets stacked to one side along with several empty oak barrels. Along the other side was a series of work benches. Some tools and equipment was scattered along them. In front of the benches were dozens of wooden crates. Directly ahead there was a wooden wall with a half open door leading deeper into the hillside.

Ellen bent over one of the crates to inspect a freshly painted stencil on side, it read: *Girardi Vineyards*. It was full. She smiled to herself. A quick inspection showed that there were many other cases were also marked *Girardi*. Among the pallets there were also several stacks of crates with different markings, including several marked *Markham Vineyards*. Many held unopened bottles of wine. Ellen leaned her shapely backside against a stack of wine crates and thoughtfully scratched her chin. It looked like Rawles was in league with the local sheriff. They were hijacking wine shipments and robbing wineries and planting the wine on local merchants. Then the sheriff raided the places along with federal agents. The local business supposedly selling the wine as well as the wineries from which it had been stolen were prosecuted and fined. When the wineries were forced to sell out to pay the fines, Rawles and the sheriff could pick up businesses and property cheap. They must have made tens of thousands, and all done with the law on their side. And worse, they probably got paid by the Feds for their tip offs.

Ellen shook her head in disgust. It was quite a plan. Too bad the Domino Lady was going to spoil it for them. Noticing several lanterns on the workbench, she lit one and moved toward the half open door. Pushing open the door with a squeak of unoiled hinges and holding the lantern ahead she entered a large tunnel. It was filled with stacks of wooden barrels lying on their sides stacked pyramid style. Rapping on several convinced Ellen they were empty. She passed down the aisle between multiple pyramids and turned a corner to the left. Ahead stretched another wide tunnel also lined with barrels.

Continuing along Ellen came to an area of shelves. Rows of horizontal half circles were cut into the shelves, obviously to hold rows of wine bottles. Holding up the lantern Ellen could see hundreds of dusty bottles on the shelves, all empty. In the light of the lantern she could also see a closed door ahead. The door opened into a storage area filled with dusty covered boxes of corks, labels and other winery paraphernalia. To the left another door opened on a dusty office. Light filtered through the boarded over windows. Here were some shipping desks and file cabinets.

Thoughtfully Ellen set the lantern down and reached for her lock picks. The door lock hadn't been turned in months so it took several minutes of work but it eventually clicked open. Opening the door and stepping out into the daylight Ellen looked around. A plan was beginning to form in her head.

Within minutes she had loaded a crate of the stolen Girardi wine into her roadster's trunk. She then rooted around and found some tools in the loading dock area. Taking hammer, a length of rope and some nails she moved into the barrel room. Working by lantern light, she went to work. She cut the rope into three lengths and nailed the ends of the ropes to some strategic items. She also used the hammer to knock away a few strategic blocks of wood. When she was finished she trailed the lengths of rope along the floor and around the corner of the barrel room. Replacing the lantern on the work bench, she left through the office but not before thoughtfully positioning a screwdriver on a desk in the office. She then relocked all the doors and headed for her car.

On the way out she drove slowly around all the buildings and down the long drive to the county road. She made note of several things on the way. She drove carefully back to town being careful of the speed limits. It wouldn't do to be stopped by policeman while carrying a crate of bootleg booze in her trunk. Upon reaching her hotel, Ellen went up to her room to rest. She was planning a busy night and tomorrow wouldn't be much better.

After a quick dinner at a quiet restaurant, Ellen drove to Rawles' house. She parked down the street and waited. The lights were on in his house but there was no sign of movement. The street was dark and parked in the shadow of a large oak tree Ellen was just a dark shadow slumped in the seat. She waited patiently. Eventually the lights in Rawles house went out and the man himself appeared on his front porch. She glanced at her watch; it was just seven thirty. She waited until the ex-DA was about of sight before swinging the black cape around her shoulders. She slipped her mask over her eyes and started her car. Easing it quietly forward she stopped directly in front of Rawles' house. She got out of the car and looked around. All was quiet. A few lights showed in nearby homes but the street was empty.

Ellen removed the crate of wine from her trunk and lugged it around behind Rawles' house. Two minutes of work and she had the back door open. She carried the crate into the kitchen and set it down. Pulling out her flashlight she commenced a search of the house. A half hour later she stood frustrated in the master bedroom. The rest of the house was empty of anything incriminating. She had hoped to find ledgers or records of Rawles illegal activities but had found nothing. This was the last room not searched.

The dresser held nothing out of the ordinary except a loaded revolver. She searched under the bed and finding nothing moved to the closet. Inside were hung several business suits and other assorted clothing. On the floor were two suitcases and a leather satchel. The suitcases were empty but when she opened the satchel she found it was filled with cash.

Pleasantly surprised she rummaged around and did a rough count. There was more than fifty thousand dollars in the satchel. The Domino Lady looked longingly at the cash but after a moment she reluctantly replaced the money in the satchel and shoved it back in the closet. She often came across money like this in her adventures. She usually kept what she needed to maintain her high flying life style and made sure the rest went to charities and other worthy projects. The money in Rawles' closet could do a lot of good but without any financial records it was the only thing tying Rawles to his illegal activities. She turned to go but at the last minute reached back into the satchel and pulled out three packets of bills. She shoved this into a pocket in her cloak as she made her way out of the bedroom.

Leaving the darkened house the Domino Lady hauled the crate of wine out into the backyard. There she quickly discovered a small wooden door that closed off an entrance under the house. She shoved the crate inside and closed the door securely. Minutes later, mask off, she was motoring back to her hotel.

Ellen spent the next day waiting. She called Barb and gave her friend a censored account of what she suspected of Rawles and the sheriff. Next she had the phone operator look up a couple of out of town phone numbers that she wrote down. She ate a quick lunch and then took a nap.

At four thirty she walked downtown from her hotel and found a phone booth in a restaurant. Inside she asked for the long distance operator. When she was connected she told the operator she wanted Sacramento, and gave her one of the numbers she had written down. There was a pause before someone finally came on the line, "Treasury Department."

Ellen glanced at her watch; it was nearly five o'clock, "Listen you better get a couple of your agents down to Napa tomorrow. There's a gang of crooks led by the sheriff and the ex-DA that are running a big bootlegging operation down there."

"What!" Who is this?"

"Never mind. Just get some people down there tomorrow, and don't trust any local cops. Like I say the sheriff is behind this. Oh, and don't forget to search the ex-DA's house. You'll find some very interesting things there."

"Listen lady, I need to know who you…" Ellen hung up the phone and left the phone booth. She whistled to herself as she walked back to her hotel. Things had been set in motion. Now it would get interesting.

At eight that night Ellen checked out of her hotel. Her bags in the car, she settled herself behind the wheel and headed north out of town. It took less than a half hour to get back to the former Markham vineyards. On the way she stopped at a filling station. While the garage attendant was filling her car and washing her windshield, she asked to use the telephone in the office. The attendant waved to her to go ahead. She had the operator connect her with the second of two numbers she had written down. When she was connected a man answered, "State Police."

"Listen, the sheriff of Napa County is running a bootlegging gang. They're meeting tonight at the bankrupt Markham Winery. They're planning another wine hi-jacking right now. If you hurry you can round them all up. Don't trust the local cops."

"Hey, who is…" Ellen hung up. She strolled casually outside and paid the attendant. As she drove away, she smiled thinking that should get things moving at the State Police barracks.

Fifteen minutes later she entered the Markham winery driveway but this time did not drive to the winery buildings. Instead she pulled off the drive into a narrow opening in the trees she had spotted earlier and drove until she was sure her car couldn't be seen from the drive. There she pulled on her cloak and mask and left the car.

Using her flashlight sparingly she made her way up the drive, past the buildings and to the office door set into the hillside. She unlocked it and entered. Rather than relocking the outside door she braced a chair up under the door knob to keep it from opening. Then using the flash she made her way through the cave to the corner of the barrel room where it turned toward the loading dock. She made sure the door into the loading area was partially open, then found a place behind a pyramid of barrels at the corner and settled down to wait.

It was dark and eerie with her flashlight off and the air was cool enough that she pulled her cloak closer about her shoulders. The time seemed to pass with agonizing slowness to the masked woman. She had to stifle a sigh of relief when she finally heard the double doors rattle outside the loading dock.

Soon a bright light shone past the half open door. A voice spoke, "Where's the truck?"

Another voice answered, "Charlie's driving it out here with Abe. They ought to be here soon."

Crouched in the darkness, one hand gripping the ropes and the other her small pistol the Domino Lady considered that. It sounded like the sheriff and Rawles were there. But if she sprang her trap now she might run into two more of the gang while getting away. Better to wait for developments. She cocked her head to hear more of the low voiced conversation.

"Say, I'm gonna take a few bottles home with me. The wife used to like Girardi wine."

This was answered by a chuckle, "Go ahead. There's plenty. Let's divide these into lots. How many places are you going to plant these on?"

"Lemma see...I've got four different places I can say are selling bootleg booze. I know their layout and can stash this stuff in their garages or barns. Tomorrow I'll call that dumb Treasury guy and tell him we're gonna make some raids. He never cares how I know. All he cares about is looking good to his bosses."

She heard another chuckle, "Well he'll certainly have plenty of people to prosecute now. Maybe we can pick up some other places cheap after the dust from the trials settles." There came the clinking of bottles and other sounds as the two conspirators moved crates around in the outer loading room.

Minutes later one of the voices spoke up, "Hear that. It sounds like the boys." There was a pause then, "Yep. There's their lights."

"Good, the sooner we get this stuff loaded the better."

The Domino Lady nodded to herself. Now she knew where everyone was. She stood up. Counting to herself she gave the newcomers another minute to get their truck parked then set down her pistol on the concrete floor of the cave and picked up the empty wine bottle she placed there earlier. She then shoved it along the floor in the dark. It hit something and bounced off it with a loud "clink!" She then grabbed up her pistol and waited.

There was a sudden silence from the outer room and a voice asked suspiciously, "What was that?"

"In there, I heard something."

Crouching down Domino Lady saw the outer door open and a band of light flood into the dark barrel room. Silhouetted in the doorway was a man. She could not make out who it was. He stepped forward holding up a flashlight, sweeping its beam across the stacks of empty barrels. She kept down but peered low around the corner. She needed both men inside the room to spring her trap. A voice from the outer room spoke, "What is it?"

"I don't see anything."

Reluctantly realizing she would have to raise the ante the Domino Lady kicked the empty barrel nearest her. The hollow thump echoed through the cave. The man at the door reacted by shining his light toward her, "There's someone here!"

Another man appeared in the doorway as the first man stepped forward. The second man also had a flashlight but in his other hand was a gun. Domino Lady stood up and leaned slightly around the corner of a stack of barrels, just enough so that the two could see movement. They yelled and plunged forward.

The Domino Lady tightened her grip on the ropes and turned to run the other way. The ropes tightened and jerked her back for a moment. Then the wooden blocks nailed to the ends of the ropes pulled loose from where they were wedged under the barrels. Without the wedges to hold them three stack of barrels rolled forward, the heavy weight of those stacked above forcing the lowest tiers outwards. There were yells of alarm from

Rawles and the Sheriff as the barrels rolled outward.

A barrel caught the sheriff in the thigh. He went sideways up and over it as it rolled under him. As he flipped he involuntarily squeezed the trigger of this revolver. The bullet hit the stone roof of the cave and ricocheted off into the darkness the bang echoing loudly through the caves. He was swept under the next rolling barrel. Rawles dropped his flashlight and jumped forward to avoid a rolling barrel but the next one hit him in the back of his thighs and he went backward over it.

The masked woman glanced back; barrels were rolling everywhere. A few had smashed into walls and broken apart. The barrel room was dark except for the glow of flashlights somewhere under piles of barrels. The outer door must have been slammed shut by a barrel's impact just as she had hoped. As she turned to run the other way, she heard a man yelling in pain.

Using her small flashlight she made her quickly along the main cave and into the office. Shoving the chair aside, she opened the outside door and leaned out. A man dressed in workman's clothing was running from a large covered truck toward the loading doors. As soon as he entered she ran forward and quickly swung the double doors shut. She had a glimpse of his shocked face before the doors slammed together. She flipped the hasp closed and slipped the screwdriver she had grabbed off the desk through the hasp, effectively locking the doors.

As she turned, a man rounded the truck running toward her. She calmly raised her pistol and fired once, the bullet plowing into the ground in front of him. He skidded to a halt in amazement as the masked woman walked toward him. She pointed the gun at him and said, "Hands Up!"

Shocked he nonetheless did as he was told. She then continued, "Turn around!" He did so. The Domino Lady then reached up under her dress and pulled a capped syringe from where it was secured against her thigh. She stepped forward and prodded the man in the back with her pistol and spoke firmly, "Don't move!" He spoke nervously, "Look lady I don't know what...Owww!" His yell was caused by the needle she plunged into his neck. She stepped back as he clapped his hand to his neck and crumpled gracefully to the ground. She wasn't worried. The fast acting drug she had injected him with had no permanent effects but would keep him unconscious for hours.

She bent and searched through the man's pants pockets quickly finding what she was looking for; a pocket knife. She opened it as she walked to the truck. She plunged the knife into a tire and it deflated with a hiss.

She then opened the door and reaching into the front of her dress removed a small black card and laid it on the driver's seat. The card was black and printed in white lettering on it were the words *Compliments of the Domino Lady*. She made her way to the two other vehicles and calmly deflated a tire on each. As she then made her way toward the darkened drive the noise of engines came to her ears. At the same time she saw light reflected off the trees lining the drive.

The Domino Lady turned and darted for the corner of the large house. She ducked around it just as car came into view moving slowly. A second car closely followed it. Before she ducked back she made out the white doors with painted insignia on them. She shook her head. It looked like the State Police were more efficient than she had counted on. Turning, she circled the house keeping it between her and the police cars as they drove past it. Leaning around the far corner she could see two officers get out of each car. Using flashlights they spread out and began examining the newly disabled vehicles. One of them quickly found the unconscious man and things got very interesting. As the officers gathered over the unconscious man she wrapped her black cloak around her and scurried quietly across the yard into some trees near the drive. From there she made her way quietly down the drive to where she had hidden her car.

Once inside her car the beautiful masked avenger bit her lip in indecision. She needed to be patient. If she left now the police would certainly hear the noise of her roadster starting up. Soon they would be too involved arresting the suspects she had left behind to chase her. On the other hand more police might show up any second. She gave it another minute before starting the roadster. She quickly backed through the trees to the drive and turned down it. At the county road she turned south and sped away. Once away from the winery she removed her mask and cape and breathed a sigh of relief.

A half hour later she was back in Napa. There she drove quietly past the small house where the Markhams lived. It was dark. She circled back and pulled up in front of the mailbox. Reaching out of the car she opened the box and shoved one of the packets of money she had taken from Rawles' house inside. She smiled and hefted the other two packets. One was earmarked for some needy charities she had in mind. The other would be used to continue her crusade. She flipped the box shut and motored quietly away and then headed north for the Girardi winery.

The next afternoon Ellen waved to Barb and her father as she drove away in her roadster. She had spent the night at the Girardis. She hadn't told much to Barb and her family; just that she had heard that good news was coming soon. Sure enough the phone had started ringing the next morning. Word was spreading quickly that the sheriff and ex-DA Rawles had been arrested. As details came in it became obvious that the two had been behind a lot of the troubles suffered by the nearby wineries. The Girardis were surprised but happy. Probably how a lot of people were going to feel, mused Ellen a she reached the state road and turned south for the long drive home.

The End

CALIFORNIA GIRLS
Part 1

The Beach Boys once sang about California Girls…well the Domino Lady definitely falls into that category. This was quite remarkable for a pulp hero of the 1930s. Not only was she a woman but she also operated out on the west coast. It was far more common for heroes to be crowded into New York City (probably couldn't go a block without bumping into a masked hero) or to work out of their own invented city. But Domino Lady and her alter ego Ellen Patrick definitely were West Coast girls. That's one of the many charms the character had for me.

I have written stories for both of the first two Domino Lady anthologies published by Airship 27. I had my trepidations about the character when I wrote the first story but had so much fun that I quickly came up with a story for volume 2. So when it became obvious that there would be a third volume, I knew I had to write a story for it.

I was born and raised in the Golden State and although I have lived in the Pacific Northwest for a very long time my wife and I still visit California from time to time. One of the areas we visit often is wine country around Napa and Sonoma to visit the many world class wineries. So when I was casting about for colorful California areas to set a new Domino Lady adventure in, Napa quickly came to mind. Another plus to this was that I could tie in Prohibition as it affected the wine industry.

While looking for background information I came across a wonderful book: *Prohibition in the Napa Valley*. It was filled with wonderful stories about the people and wineries there and how they survived Prohibition. This book was a fund of wonderful plot ideas, several of which I use. So all the improbable I things I write about in *Over a Barrel* like dehydrated grape juice blocks, selling sacramental wine and the Feds fining and driving wineries out of business actually happened.

One further note; all of you familiar with California may wonder about my use of State Police rather than the famous California Highway Patrol. During my research I found out that the Highway Patrol was still a very young agency at the time of this story. It was actually founded in 1929 with "Traffic Officers" to patrol the roads of the Golden State. The State Police were long established. In fact the State Police existed until 1995 when they officially merged with the Highway Patrol. Who knew?

Anyway all this seemed tailor made for a Domino Lady adventure. So

I came up with a plot and away I went. The writing went well at first but then bogged down. The first part of the story was all right but then there was a major change of scene that seemed jarring. Also, since Napa is not a particularly glamorous area like Los Angeles or San Francisco the story didn't seem as exciting as my first stories. The worst part was it was way too short. It wasn't going to fit the needs of a Domino Lady anthology.

I stopped writing and stewed over this for a couple of days unsure of what to do to save the story. Then I read an Airship update from Ron Fortier where he talked about the "older format" that they used in their early anthologies. This was interesting. I wrote Ron and asked for a clarification. He explained that before I came on board as writer for them, Airship 27 occasionally published a few shorter stories in their anthologies. Ah-haa!

I had already figured out that if I cut out the awkward ending I could make my Domino Lady story into a short, tight adventure; unfortunately far too short for a standard anthology. But when Ron told me he was returning to occasional use of their early format I knew *Over a Barrel* would work perfectly. He agreed; so I went back to work.

I shortened the story, streamlined the ending and even added some local Bay area history and landmarks for flavor. When finished, I was pleased. I believe *Over a Barrel* is a fine little short Domino Lady adventure. There isn't too much mystery in it but you could say that about any Domino Lady adventure. The strength of her stories is how she takes down the bad guys, and that worked out just fine in this story. I even used an underground wine cellar I toured last year in Napa as a back drop for the final encounter Domino Lady has with the bad guys.

So I had a good short story for the Airship...now I just had to come up with a second matching short story since Ron wanted two shorts to full the spot of one longer story. That was going to take some thought. It took a bit but I finally came up with something good, but that is another story...

THE DOMINO LADY'S SCANDAL
By Brad Mengel

*L*ike many of the Domino Lady's adventures, this one started with a phone call. The caller was Emilio Romani, Hollywood heartthrob inviting her to lunch. Ellen Patrick frequently appeared in the social pages of Hollywood Gossip rags. She'd been photographed on the arm of more than one handsome leading man. So, a call from the latest heartthrob came as no surprise.

She'd met Romani at Neville Sinclair's bash the week before. The handsome young man had first come to the world's attention in The Gypsy, a year or so earlier. Through the grapevine Ellen had heard that "The Man with the Million Dollar Smile" was going to be throwing a lavish party soon. He was celebrating the success of his new film Son of the Gypsy. Women around the world swooned when he flashed those pearly whites on the screen.

Legend had it that a studio head saw the effect of Emilio's grin on a waitress at the diner and immediately offered him a million-dollar contract. Perhaps Romani had met his match as Ellen Patrick's own cupid bow lips had been known to drive more than one man crazy.

Ellen looked a vision as she walked into the restaurant, heads turned as the waiter showed her to her seat. Ellen told her guide that she was waiting for someone. He brought her a carafe of water and walked away.

She was only alone for a couple of minutes before her companion slipped into the chair opposite her. His fedora was pulled low and he was wearing sun cheaters over his eyes. The waiter scurried over to take his coat and hat. Emilio pulled off the glasses. The waiter's eyes widened as he recognized the movie star and he nearly sprinted away from the table.

"Probably off to get his autograph book." Ellen suggested.

Emilio laughed, a deep throaty laugh that sent tingles along Ellen's spine. "He's probably calling Louella Parsons. By the time the story reaches her column, I'll be declaring my eternal love and proposing."

"I thought you were cavorting on the beach with your last co-star I read." Ellen said wryly.

"Well I heard from Alan Swann that if she reports over 100 proposals for you in a year in Lolly Parsons' column she sends you a bottle of champers for Christmas. Swanny of course gets two bottles every year." Emilio flashed his smile at her.

"So, you're trying for a case?" Ellen queried.

Another peal of laughter came from the darkly handsome actor.

The waiter returned to the table. He tried to pour some water for the movie star but his hand shook far too much. The movie star and the socialite exchanged glances.

"W-w-would you like a m-m-menu?" stammered out the man. "or the s-s-specials?"

"Just the menus," said Ellen.

The waiter promptly fled from the table.

"You get that reaction often?" Ellen enquired. "He was fine while he served me."

"A few ladies have fainted, but this is a first for me."

The pair engaged in brief chit chat before the waiter returned and literally threw the menus at the table. Ellen looked at the waiter in disbelief it was almost as if he was scared of the Hollywood actor. Not the usual "nervous to meet you" but actual fear. Before Ellen could ponder this unusual behavior further, they were joined by another three men.

Big and burly, the trio wore their dark suits and fedoras like a uniform. That was not too surprising given that the suits were issued by LAPD. As The Domino Lady, Ellen had found it particularly useful to be able to recognize a plain clothes officer of the law.

The leader was a blonde man. He reached into his pocket and pulled out his identification. The other two acted in near perfect unison and three gold shields all flashed simultaneously.

"Detective Anderson." The leader identified himself. His voice carried the slightest hint of the sing song tones of the old country suggesting that he had emigrated here while quite young. Anderson cocked his head to the left indicating the red head "Mulhoon" and then the right "and Schulz."

Mulhoon had the fair skin of a true son of Erin and the California sun had peppered his face with freckles. Schulz was completely bald and had that look of Germanic efficiency but was probably known as Dutchy having hidden his nationality during the Great War. LAPD had sent a veritable League of Nations.

"Mr. Romani," continued Anderson, "there has been an allegation made against you and we would like you to join us for a quick chat at the station."

Ellen followed Romani's eyes as they darted around looking for an escape. He'd faced a comparable situation in "The Memoirs of Casanova" where he outmatched three overweight jilted husbands all the while blowing kisses to his paramour while swinging to safety on the chandelier and he might try something like that here. Ellen had seen and quite enjoyed the movie but her experience as the Domino Lady told her it wasn't going to work here. In this case, these were not stuntmen following a script and helping the star look good.

Ellen looked up and saw that there was a hanging light fitting in the cafe just at the right distance for a swashbuckling actor to leap from the table and sail over the police officers' heads. Ellen could see about a dozen ways this could go badly.

Emilio was reaching for his drink, which if Ellen recalled the movie correctly was to be thrown into Anderson's face. It looked like Schulz had seen the movie too and was reaching into his jacket for the pistol he wore under his armpit.

Ellen had to defuse this quickly or it was looking rather fatal for the movie star. She reached out and put her hand on Romani's arm. "Now darling, there's no reason to worry I'm sure these police officers are just here to clear this matter right up."

Ellen didn't believe one word she was saying given her previous encounters with the California political machine and how they controlled the police force. She made a note in the back of her mind to contact Paul Cathern or Roge McCone for more information about these three, once she got past this situation.

Ellen put on her sweetest smile, "Oh Detective Anderson, which station house will you be taking Mr. Romani? Just so I can tell his lawyer where to meet him."

If the trio of thugs with badges had any plans for a phone book interrogation, hopefully the swift arrival of a lawyer should put a crimp in any nefarious plans they might have. Anderson grunted out a nearby station and herded the movie star out of the restaurant.

Ellen had formed a network of people she had met during her time at Berkeley including a law student, Jack Moore. Moore had been shy and studious and been having trouble with speaking in front of people. His roommate was dating a friend of Ellen's. The butter haired beauty had been consulted to help bring him out of his shell. Ellen had taken him to dinner and built up his confidence. He'd been able to pass his classes and later the bar.

A couple of years back he'd set up shop in Los Angeles under the name of J.C. Moore. Ellen had run into him and his wife Lacey at a political fundraiser where he had given her his card. Ellen had memorized the number, if she was ever captured or exposed as Domino Lady, he was to be her lawyer.

The socialite made her way to the courtesy phone and dialed Moore's number. Moore's strong baritone voice came on the line.

"Jack, darling, my good friend Emilio Romani has been taken to the police station and I think he needs a lawyer."

"Ellen, I'd do anything for you and if Lacey found out that I had the chance to meet 'the million-dollar smile' and passed it up, why she might just divorce me. She's going to be sore with you that you didn't tell her that you knew him."

Ellen and Lacey had become fast friends and served on the boards of several charities. Lacey Moore was a huge fan of Emilio Romani and she and Ellen had seen all his movies. "Well I only just met him and had the police not taken him away, you know that my first call would have been to your lovely wife."

Ellen rattled off the station and gave the lawyer a brief description of what happened and mentioned the trio of detectives Anderson, Schulz and Mulhoon.

Moore let loose a whistle "The Trident. The dirtiest cops this side of Chicago. Ellen, you need to let me handle this. I'm heading to the station; I'll call you once it's done."

With that the call had ended and Ellen returned the phone to the hook. While her friend had basically told her to stay out of this, Ellen was not one to sit on the sidelines. That call to Cathern had become a priority now; she wanted to know more about these crooked detectives. But there was one lead that she wanted to follow up before she went home.

The waiter's reaction to Emilio was more than nerves or the excitement of meeting a movie star. And the call they had speculated about was not to Lolly Parson's gossip column but a tip off to the cops.

Ellen looked around for the nervous waiter but the man was nowhere to be seen. She flagged down another member of staff. The young brunette waitress smiled in response to Ellen's query. "I shouldn't tell you this but he's taking a break out in the back alley having a gasper."

The blonde socialite thanked the waitress and gave the young lady a hefty tip. She then made her way to the ladies' room. But this trip was not to "powder her nose". Ellen had brought her special bag, the one with the secret compartment, today. She opened the hidden pocket and pulled out a slinky white dress and a similar black cape. Ellen then removed the floral print dress she had worn today. The hot California air kissed her alabaster skin. A trickle of sweat ran down her kissable neck before trailing down to her décolletage.

Ellen threw on the white dress which hugged and caressed her curves, leaving very little to the imagination. The cape wrapped around her kissable shoulders. Next came the domino mask and her trusty gun and a syringe of knock out drug which she tucked into her garters. The Domino Lady was ready for action.

The Domino Lady moved swiftly and silently to the back exit and eased open the door peering through the gap. The waiter was there alone and he was taking the last few puffs of his hand rolled cigarette. A few loose clumps of tobacco lay on the ground around the waiter's feet indicating just how much his hands were shaking as he filled the paper.

The man appeared much calmer but his eyes were darting around the alley. As he took a long drag on the cigarette, the Domino Lady burst through the door. The waiter released his grip on the butt and nearly inhaled the lit cigarette. He spat and a hacking cough racked his body allowing the buxom vigilante to cross the distance between them.

With her trusty gun in hand, Domino Lady covered the waiter. "Who wanted Romani out of the way?"

"Puta." Spat the waiter between gasps as he clenched a fist.

"That's no way to treat a lady. I want the information now or I'll shoot off your pinky toe." Domino Lady was an excellent shot and could shoot the nail off the pinky toe at this distance.

The fist unclenched as the waiter stifled another cough, recognizing when he had no other choice. "There was a call, no name given; gravelly voice offered me a sawbuck to call the cops if Romani turned up here. One of my amigos got a similar offer."

"How were you to get this payoff?" Domino Lady asked as she kept the man covered, she could sense that he was getting his confidence back and his machismo would mean he'd have to try and attack her.

"I'm not telling you," he said as he telegraphed the punch.

Domino Lady avoided the clumsy blow and smacked the butt of her gun on the back of his head. The waiter landed face first in some food scraps that missed the trash can but he had already lost consciousness.

Knowing the man would be missed soon, Domino Lady retreated to the bathroom and emerged as Ellen Patrick. She left the restaurant and climbed into her car. She sat for a few moments. The police station was nearby but if Moore saw her he was sure to be very sore at her. Given her long-term plans for Moore, it was in Ellen's best interests to keep him on her side so she returned home.

Ellen's first job was to call Paul Cathern. The special investigator for the

Sheriff's Office was out on a job. Ellen left a message to him to call her. Her call to Roge McCone was similarly unsuccessful. She'd reached his secretary Christina, a red head with designs of matrimony on her boss. The other woman was wildly jealous of Ellen and would routinely withhold her messages. The only woman Christina hated more than Ellen Patrick was the Domino Lady.

Having made her calls, there was little more to do than wait. Ellen changed out of the dress she wore to lunch and kicked off her shoes, threw on a kimono she had purchased during her tour of the Orient. Normally she liked to wear nothing under it and feel the silk on her alabaster skin but as there was chance that she might have to leave quickly so she retained her underwear and stockings. She had bought the robe on the same day that she received the telegram that her father had been murdered. That was the worst day of her life. Owen Patrick was a God to young Ellen.

After her mother died, Owen had moved heaven and Earth not only to raise her but had worked tirelessly to thwart the California political machine that was threating to corrupt and destroy the great State of California. He'd been killed trying to make the world better for her and in return Ellen had sacrificed much to further his work. It was that day in the Orient that she had formed the plan to adopt a disguise and work outside the system to bring down the men who had killed her father. It was the quiet moments like this that she wondered what her life might have been like had her father not died, would she have married any of the number of men she had met since his death? Might she have had children? But this was all idle speculation. Ellen had become the Domino Lady and was committed to bringing down the political machine and helping her friends.

It was at that point she heard the special chimes she had installed in her phone, as she found the regular bell far too obtrusive. "Hello," she invited her caller in the most seductive tone.

"Ellen," came Moore's voice. "This doesn't look good. I've secured bail for Romani but I don't think he should be alone. I have a big trial starting tomorrow and I don't want Lacey to see her heartthrob like this. Can you meet me at his house?"

The lawyer gave a very exclusive address in the Hollywoodland estate up in the hills. Ellen immediately agreed. After ending that conversation Ellen then rang down to the concierge and arranged for her car to be brought to the front door.

With that arranged the young socialite slid out of her kimono as she walked to her boudoir and selected a lovely ruby red dress with matching Cuban heeled shoes. Ellen was just reapplying Sensual Scarlet lipstick to her cupid bow lips as the phone played its tinkling melody. The concierge was on the other end advising her car was at the curb.

Ellen grabbed her special handbag and left her apartment. It was only a matter of moments before she was behind the wheel heading for the Hollywood hills.

One of Romani's neighbors was John Sanford, a local councilman whose name had come up in the periphery of several of the Domino Lady's exploits, so Ellen had no problem with finding the address. The movie star lived in a mansion with a palm lined driveway that ended with a large turning circle. Ellen parked her roadster at the top of the circle beside the front door.

The door flew open. "Thank God, you are here. The lawyer man he said that you called him. Thank the heavens that you did, those were not good men." Romani said in a rapid-fire blur of words. Gone was the suave movie star with the million dollar looks. His hair was unkempt and it looked as though Romani had aged nearly a decade in the last few hours.

He was babbling, his world had been shattered. In this town, movie stars were used to being treated like gods and when trouble arose the studios stepped in to prevent any damage to their reputation. Ellen had heard rumors of murders being covered up, pay offs to disgruntled lovers and strategic marriages to hide certain sexual escapades. It was rare for an actor to be arrested. Why Ellen could count on the fingers of one hand the big-name actors and actresses who had been arrested and the number that actually made their way to the courtroom, could be counted on her cute button nose.

Romani had been blindsided by his studio; they never would have let him be arrested and certainly not by cops nicknamed the Trident. Romani was worth far too much to the studio for him to be taken for the longest ride into the desert. This wasn't a hit; someone was trying to send a message to the studio.

Ellen took the man by the hand and led him back into the house. "Don't worry. Mr. Moore will take care of everything. And I'm here to help. What you need is a good shower to wash off the police station."

"Yes, that's what I'll do." He said slightly slurring his words as Ellen shut the front door.

The Hollywood star was like a zombie as Ellen led him through the mansion to find a bathroom. Romani was so overwhelmed that he could barely function and was no help in finding his room. Luckily, Ellen had been in a few of these big houses and was able to deduce the likely location of the master bedroom.

Once in the en suite bathroom, she spun the taps and let the water heat up. She turned her back and ordered Romani to get out of his clothes. The little devil on her shoulder offered the suggestion take a peek at the little Romani but it seemed too much like taking advantage of the man. Once she heard the shower curtain pulled, she grabbed his discarded clothes and dumped them in the laundry chute.

She shut the bathroom door, retreating to the bedroom and into the walk-in wardrobe. A low whistle escaped her lips; the room was larger than her master bedroom. While half the hanging space was devoted to a variety of frocks and other items of lady's apparel, the other half was full of the most fashionable men's clothes. During a trip to New York she'd met Theodore Marley Brooks, a lawyer who regularly topped the best dressed lists. This collection of clothes would be enough to make him weep.

Ellen picked out a simple outfit of a light cotton blue shirt and tan chinos with the appropriate undergarments. After laying them on the bed, she rapped on the door. "Time to get out, mister." She nearly added that she still had to have a shower, just as she did for her father. The old man would often come up with ideas in there and would lose track of time. Ellen smiled at the memory.

A couple of minutes later, Emilio appeared in a cloud of steam with a towel wrapped around his waist. Ellen took a moment to drink in his finely sculpted chest and abs. Michelangelo might well have used Emilio to model for his David. The steam made his hair frizz in the most adorable way.

"I'll wait in the sitting room for you." Ellen said as she regained use of her tongue. She'd spied the small room down the hall as she was looking for the master bedroom.

It was only a few moments before she was joined by the now dressed movie star. He still seemed distracted. His hair had not been brushed and the shirt was only half tucked in and a couple of buttons had been mis-buttoned in the wrong holes. He wavered on his feet like he was about to collapse. "Shanks for…." He started, slurring his words and trailing off his sentence.

They had not had time to order drinks at lunch and local police station was especially not known for serving booze even before Prohibition. He hadn't smelt of anything when she arrived so it was unlikely that he grabbed a drink or three to soothe his nerves when he got home.

It might be drugs, Hollywood was full of them. Several of the men in her circles had offered Ellen cocaine and opium at parties. Ellen had always refused; often she was at the party as a cover for the Domino Lady and needed a clear head and even if she wasn't there on a mission, she never used drugs.

Ellen took a closer look at Emilio. While she was no Monk Mayfair or Fergus MacMurdie, Ellen was a skilled chemist. She'd concocted the knockout drug used by The Domino Lady, so she was familiar with the effects of many of the recreational drugs used in Hollywood. Romani's pupils weren't dilated, his eyes were a little bloodshot but that was likely from the harsh lights used on the film sets, Ellen had seen drug users and their eyes were far more bloodshot. There were no obvious puncture marks on his arms. While some users injected between the toes to keep the marks hidden, there were no needles or other clues to drug use. The most obvious thing was shellshock. The best treatment would be to try and get his life back to some sort of normality.

"Let's go down to the kitchen and get you something to eat. After all I still owe you lunch." Ellen said as she grabbed him by the wrist.

Ellen led the man down the stairs and through the house into the kitchen. Emilio sat at the small kitchen table as Ellen looked through the pantry and the ice chest. There were slim pickings but Ellen found the makings of a peanut-butter and jelly sandwich. Ellen quickly spread the bread and cut off the crusts before making little triangles.

Emilio stared blankly at the plate in front of him. "I should have done something about that phone call."

"What call would that be?" Ellen asked, her instincts alert for a clue.

"It was a week or so back. I'd just gotten back from a party thrown by Satan Devlin, we'd just finished shooting The Daredevils and were blowing off steam. I may have had one or two sips of some Canadian drinks and I was a little tipsy."

While talking, his hands picked up the little triangle sandwich. As he stopped talking he popped the sandwich in his mouth and chewed for a few minutes.

"The phone was ringing as I walked through the door. The voice on the other end said that I should talk to Harold about getting ten thousand bucks."

Harold would be Harold Stevenson the head of Phoenix Studios, where Emilio was under contract. Ellen had the dubious pleasure of his company in the past; he offered to make her a star if she starred on his casting couch

"...his eyes were a little bloodshot..."

first. Ellen declined but her friend Dottie had not. Once Dottie had made a name for herself as an actress, other studios tried to woo her away from Phoenix but Stevenson threated to release the film.

Dottie had confided in her friend Ellen Patrick but the Domino Lady was the one to act on it. It was a mission that nearly ended in disaster as Stevenson had caught her in the act and she found herself tied to the casting couch and being threatened with a riding crop. It was only in his haste to set up the camera, Stevenson had poorly tied the knots and Domino Lady slipped out of her ties.

Ellen had been keeping an eye on the studio head and he had seemed to be keeping to the straight and narrow, the Domino Lady's lesson meant he couldn't sit for the best part of a week. Now it appeared that there were more shady deals afoot.

"Did you talk to Harold?" Ellen asked.

"I didn't, I thought the call was a….a pink elephant, imagined while I was drunk. It's happened before. I seem to recall being something of a smart mouth to Johnny, he said his name was Johnny. Until today, I would have sworn it was a dream." Emilio dropped his head to the table. A sob racked his frame before he continued. "The police arrested me. They said it was statutory rape. I ain't never forced anyone to be with me. The thought makes me sick."

Ellen recalled hearing that Emilio had gotten into a brawl on set when some frisky lothario refused to take no for an answer from one of the Gypsy girls. Of course, in true Hollywood fashion, there were several versions including a knife fight, a duel with swords and an ambush with a pistol. There was even a story that the evil eye had been placed.

"Statutory rape means that the girl was too young to give consent. Much like a child cannot sign a contract." Ellen explained.

"I'd never interfere with a child." Emilio slammed his fist on the table.

"You may not have realized that she was too young, especially if she was wearing makeup."

Emilio thought for a moment. "True, there was one young lady who appeared here in my bedroom. She really didn't have anywhere to carry her birth certificate, and I didn't even think to ask for it."

"Did she give you a name?"

"I barely had the chance to say hello." A ghost of a smile played on Emilio's lips.

"Or it could have been at some party. It's easy for a young girl to sneak into one of them." Ellen mused. "Not that I ever did that myself."

Emilio looked over the table at her. "I definitely never saw you at any of

Valentino's parties that he threw every Friday night at the Hyperion hotel."

Ellen's father had taught her to play poker including keeping a poker face, but a flicker of surprise crossed her face.

"Don't worry it'll be our secret," the actor said. "I used to work as a waiter in the hotel."

Just then the phone rang. Its jangling shattered the mood and Emilio looked like a startled rabbit ready to flee.

Ellen picked up the phone. "Emilio Romani's residence."

"Is he home yet?" asked a gravelly voice.

Ellen signaled the actor over. "I'll put him on."

Ellen tilted the handset so that she could listen in on the conversation.

"You should have listened; the price is now fifty thousand for this to all go away. You tell that double dealer Stevenson that we had a deal." Something about the voice seemed off, almost as if Johnny was faking the gravelly tone.

"If you give me any of your sass it'll be a hundred grand." The gravel dropped out for a couple of words. Ellen wondered if she had heard the voice before but with only a couple of words it was impossible to tell.

"I will call back tomorrow at the same time." Ellen glanced down at her pearl encrusted silver watch and took note of the time. She would be back again to confront Johnny.

The line died in Ellen's ear as she felt Emilio begin to shake. "I can't go and see Harold. He'll kill me!"

"Calm down, I can deal with him. We've had dealings in the past and I'm sure I can wrap him around my little finger."

"You don't understand, he's vicious and he's threatened to horsewhip me in the past." Emilio screeched in terror.

Ellen suggested they move to the living room to distract the actor. He followed her but he was still distracted by the horrors he imagined at the hands of the studio head.

It was obvious to Ellen that Emilio was on the verge of a nervous breakdown. She reached into the secret pocket of her bag and retrieved a syringe of her special knockout formula. Like Mandrake taught her she palmed the needle so that the movie star had no idea what was coming. As she reassured Emilio, patting him on the shoulder she injected him with the drug. The effect was normally quick but with Emilio it was nearly instantaneous. His eyes almost snapped shut as he became limp. Ellen arranged him comfortably on the couch and covered him with one of the throw rugs. The drugs should keep him out for a couple of hours at which point

Ellen expected him to move into a natural sleep.

With Emilio taken care of, the Domino Lady had a call to make. Ellen reached into her bag again and pulled out the white dress, black cape and the domino mask that made up the Domino Lady's outfit. Ellen pulled off her red dress and stood for a moment in her lingerie. A peal of laughter escaped her lips. If she ever imagined undressing in front of one of the handsomest and most eligible movie stars in Hollywood, it certainly wouldn't have been like this. But then again, the life of the Domino Lady was certainly not the life she envisioned before that fateful trip to the Orient. But now Ellen couldn't imagine any other life. The thrill of the hunt, matching wits with criminals, the adrenaline rush, Ellen couldn't give that up and settle down to an ordinary life.

It was the work of a few seconds to don the curve hugging dress that sent men's imaginations into overdrive; wrap the black cape over her kissable shoulders and put on the black domino mask. Her brown eyes shone with excitement through the mask as she checked her equipment. A supply of knockout needles, the trick flower that shot a spray of knockout gas, the trusty pistol and a heavy sap. She tucked the latter two into her décolletage.

It was unlikely that there was any threat to Emilio while she was gone but the Domino Lady decided to be cautious and lock the house up. She borrowed Emilio's keys to return to the house.

Darkness had fallen as she left the house. It was time for the Domino Lady to prowl. Domino Lady leapt into her car and drove into the night. Luckily Stevenson didn't live too far away. The lights were on as Domino Lady drove past and she spotted a single car in the driveway. She had hoped the producer would be spending a night on the town when she arrived but it looked like Stevenson was entertaining his newest signing. To the side of Stevenson's property was an apple orchard. The car fit neatly between the trees and Domino Lady settled in to wait for Stevenson's guest to depart.

When Ellen was a young girl she didn't like to wait, she wanted everything now. At least a month before her birthday and Christmas she would pester her parents for her present. She'd like to think that age and maturity had taught the value of patience but it had been her father. He had taken her on a hunting trip. It was just after the death of her mother. He gave her a hunting rifle and showed her how to shoot safely. The first bird she saw, Ellen pulled the trigger not even taking the time to aim. The shot blasted out and hit nothing scaring off every animal in a mile. Owen Patrick could have gotten angry and Ellen was expecting him to explode at the loss of a day's hunting. Ellen saw her father as some type of god and since the death of her mother she had become even more devoted to her sole surviving parent. Ellen's greatest fear was letting down her father. But Owen's reaction surprised her.

"Lesson one. Always aim and be sure of your prey. You did better than I did on my first hunting trip. I had been carrying the rifle over my shoulder like a soldier and shot it straight up in the air."

"Was Grandpa angry with you?" Ellen had asked, recalling the rather fierce old man.

"No, he was giving me the same lessons I'm teaching you. Be patient and you will get your prey."

So, the Domino Lady waited. Nearly an hour later, the front door opened and Stevenson escorted a young brunette out. The older man looked the picture of avuncular care as he opened the car door for the young lady and gave her a peck on the cheek. He waved cordially as she drove off.

While the older man appeared kind and likable, the young woman looked appalled even at this distance. The Domino Lady made a note to destroy Stevenson's film collection again.

Stevenson strode back into his house with a spring in his step as he kicked the door shut with his heel. It was another thirty minutes before the lights turned off in the house. And Domino Lady waited the balance of the hour before she made her move. From past experience she knew that Stevenson gave his domestic staff the night off when he was "casting", so Domino Lady only had to worry about the studio head. She wrapped the strap of her handbag around her wrist.

The Domino Lady flitted across the grounds like the ghost of sins past racing to visit an unrepentant sinner. She moved directly to the window she had used in her last visit. The broken latch had not been fixed. Of course, when she originally broke it, Ellen did it in such a way that it was difficult to detect.

Unsurprisingly the room had changed little since she was there last time. Domino Lady moved stealthily through the house to Stevenson's study. Domino Lady had remembered the combination of the safe from last time she was there but it no longer worked. It was to be expected but it never hurt to try.

The gloves were off as Domino Lady began to crack the safe, she'd picked up several tips from Jimmie Gray when she had met him on board the ship from the Orient. Ellen had left a pair of earrings in the captain's safe and the captain was too busy to retrieve them for her. Jimmie was the heir to the Graylock Safe Company and she watched him as he had opened the safe and retrieved her earrings. She twirled the dial with her ear against the safe listening to the tumblers. Minutes ticked by as she heard them fall into place one by one.

She turned the handle and pulled open the door. There must have been nearly a quarter of a million dollars on the bottom shelf, more than enough to pay off Johnny, make a donation to a home for unwed mothers and help fund the activities of the Domino Lady. The money quickly disappeared into her bag.

The top shelf had over twenty reels of film. Domino Lady grabbed the closest one and pulled her penlight from the handbag. She held the film to the light. She wanted to be sure that she wasn't burning a copy of the studio's latest magnum opus.

Within several frames there were scenes that definitely wouldn't have passed the Hays Office. The next would have given William Hays a heart attack. There was no danger of burning anything Stevenson could have released to theatres. Domino Lady took the bin from under Stevenson's desk. The bin still showed the scorch marks from the last time she burnt Stevenson's dirty film collection.

She rummaged in her bag and found her Zippo lighter. A flame leapt from the lighter with the first turn of the flint wheel. The strip of film instantly ignited when it came in contact with the fire. The flaming film was dropped into the bin where it was joined by the other reels.

The volatile chemicals in the film stock soon had flames leaping out of the bin. Domino Lady thought that her fellow vigilantes on the east coast had it easier, with the large fireplaces in the houses over there. They were less likely to burn the house down. After the initial inferno, the flames soon died down and the young avenger felt safe to leave the room.

She pulled her pistol and made her way to the master bedroom. Even if she didn't know where this room was she would have quickly found it by following the rumbling snores coming from the house's owner. Owen Patrick had been a loud snorer but Stevenson made her father sound like a handsaw compared to a buzz saw. As she walked into the room, Stevenson spoke, "Oh darlin' it's not even my birthday."

The Domino Lady froze. Her pistol was aimed to make a non-lethal shot. Sweat beaded on her forehead in the eternity it took for Stevenson to roll over and resume snoring. Her finger came away from the trigger; Stevenson had been talking in his sleep, no doubt dreaming of some starlet. It did give the Domino Lady an idea.

She returned to Stevenson's private studio and grabbed a couple of his props. She returned to the room and set to work. The bedside lamp cast a dim light over the scene. It was touch and go a couple of times but the producer was in a deep sleep after his previous nocturnal exertions. Domino Lady took the feather she had found downstairs and began to tickle Stevenson's nose.

The producer snorted and came awake. He found his hands and feet bound to the bed ends. He looked around in a panic before his eyes locked onto the bountiful curves of the Domino Lady. The panic subsided as a wave of lust surged through his body.

"Oh Darlin', it's not even my birthday." No-one had ever accused the producer of originality. He wore the giant grin of a man whose dreams had come true. A masked woman breaking into his room to tie him up and have her wanton way with him. The panic returned as he finally spotted the pistol in Domino Lady's hand. That little detail was not part of his fantasy. Whips and riding crops, yes. Guns, no. Guns caused bad pain, the producer had been shot in the Great War and he had no aspirations to repeat that very unpleasant sensation. As the sleepy dullness receded from his mind with his lustful thoughts, the producer's keen and shrewd brain finally roared into action and recognized his captor. The Domino Lady.

Their last meeting had started well for Stevenson. He'd found the curvaceous adventuress rummaging in his safe. He'd grabbed one of his many, many awards and knocked her cold. The unmasking of the Domino Lady would have made him a fortune. He tied her up and was setting up the camera to film the reveal when she escaped. He had taken her place on the couch and one of his own riding crops had been used on his back before he passed out. He'd awoken untied to find all of his blackmail films had been burnt to a cinder and the money in his safe gone.

The pain on his back had helped during the negotiations with Brigadier General Williams to bring his life story to the screen. The General had liked his ramrod straight posture and sold him the rights. The General had then slapped him on the back. It took all of Stevenson's willpower to not scream in agony.

The producer had vowed to get his revenge on the sultry vigilante but he wasn't above profiting from the woman. He was currently casting for Mistress Masque, a film serial to rival that of Republic Studios and would bring back the glory days of Pearl White or Helen Holmes. Women tied to logs headed for saws, tied to train tracks and tied up in a building about to explode, each week the writers would create a new torture for the heroine. J.P. McGowan was signed on to direct. There was a lot of interest in this serial. Indeed, the young lady he'd auditioned tonight had been very keen on the role. Most people in Los Angeles had heard rumors about a woman fighting crime and corruption so it was almost free advertising and help recoup the money she stole from him.

Only in Stevenson's wildest dreams and worst nightmares did he ever think that he would encounter the actual Domino Lady again. This encounter definitely fell into the latter category; he wasn't supposed to be tied up.

"So, Stevenson, it appears that you ignored my very strongly worded advice from my last visit. I had to set another fire and fine you all the money in your safe. But that was not why I paid you a visit tonight so if you tell me everything I want to know there will be no other penalties." Domino Lady's voice had a cruel, hard edge to it. The way she said penalties caused the scars on his back to throb a little in pain.

Stevenson's lips had dried out and stuck together, he nearly tore the skin off them as he begged. "What do you want to know?"

"I hear that you've had contact with an individual called Johnny, with a gravelly voice."

Stevenson's eyes widened, Johnny was not general knowledge. Stevenson had heard from Jack Warner that the gravel voiced fixer never interacted with the stars only with the men behind the scenes. He had dealt with the man in the past, but their last exchange had been somewhat acrimonious. The fixer had made some crazy claim that Emilio Romani was to be charged with statutory rape and that it would take ten thousand to make it go away. Stevenson had never paid more than four thousand for the services before and he would be damned before he paid such extortionate rates.

"I-I ain't never heard of Johnny," Stevenson lied badly.

Domino Lady poked her gun into his ribs. "That's not what he said, and your Brooklyn comes out when you lie."

She could see the producer's rat cunning brain spinning furiously to prepare a story to get out of this predicament. Stevenson blurted "Oh you mean the fixer, I never remembered his name. I never knew him if he ever got caught doing something illegal."

That may not have been the whole truth, but Domino Lady recognized that there was enough for her to work with. "Let me guess your fixer asked too much money to make Emilio's charges go away and you were prepared

"What do you want to know?"

to sacrifice him to save a few dollars?"

"I didn't believe it, that kid could charm the panties off a nun. He didn't rape anyone."

"Well your fixer threw him to the Trident."

The producer blanched at the mention of the three dirty cops Johnny used as his bag men. He'd met all three several times and he still got the shudders fearing they might sap him just for practice. What they might do to someone they had orders to hurt. Well, that thought caused him to lose control of his bladder.

Domino Lady saw the spreading pool of urine. "Don't worry, one of my agents saw the arrest and arranged for a lawyer. "

While the Domino Lady worked alone it never hurt to spread a little disinformation.

"Oh, thank God!" Stevenson declared. "I never thought that gravel voiced bottom feeder would hurt the talent. Romani was my new Valentino I needed him to make a ton of movies."

"Worried about your cash cow, how sweet," Domino Lady's voice dripped with sarcasm.

"It's not like that," protested the producer. "Well maybe a little but I like the kid and he's a natural on the screen. He needs to act."

"Which is why you threatened to horsewhip him."

If the producer had anything left in his bladder he may have released it, if the look on his face was anything to go by. "That was a minor disciplinary matter. He was partying with Devlin, he's the best camera man in town which is why I keep using him but he keeps dragging the talent into trouble. I told Emilio to stay away from Devlin or I'd penalize him."

"Just like I said I'd penalize you if I ever found you making casting films again."

Stevenson swallowed a large gulp.

"A penalty I'm willing to forego for information on Johnny the Fixer. Think of it as a one-time only reminder to reform and treat your stars better."

"I never met the man, he always sent the three goon cops to do his dirty work. He always calls me, I don't even have a number but he always knew when one of the stars was in trouble. I don't know anything more." The producer spoke so fast that the Domino Lady nearly couldn't follow.

It seemed that the Trident was her only lead now. The Domino Lady was a woman of her word she did not castrate the slimy producer with a well-placed bullet, this time. She did however inject him with her knock out formula and left him tied on his urine-soaked bed for the maid to find in the morning.

Domino Lady retreated back through the house and back through the window of the spare bedroom. Before long she had returned to her car. Domino Lady removed her mask ready to drive back to Emilio's house when a shudder ran down her spine.

Ellen Patrick did not believe in the supernatural but a number of soldiers, sailors and police had told her stories of some sixth sense warning them of unseen and unknown dangers. This chill down her spine seemed to one of those instances and she took advantage of the quiet of the orchard to completely change back into Ellen Patrick before she tore down the road back to Emilio Romani's house. According to her watch he should be awaking in the next quarter hour or so and Ellen wanted to be there for that. Ellen quickly changed and jumped into the driver's seat. Her car roared down the road, her blonde hair streaming behind her as she raced around the bends.

As she pulled into the driveway of Romani's house she spotted a man knocking at the door. Getting closer she recognized city councilman John Sanford. Sanford was so intent on knocking on his neighbor's door that he seemed oblivious to the arrival of Ellen's roadster. When Ellen tapped him on the shoulder the councilor near leapt out of his very expensive Italian loafers.

While Ellen was familiar with the councilman this was the first time she had seen him face to face. Oh, she had seen him from a distance at various political fundraisers, but she had never been introduced. The councilman looked appraisingly at her. Not the usual looks of the wolves, that only drank in her delectable curves going no deeper than under her clothes. No, Sanford's gaze went much deeper cutting right through her and seeming to peer into her very soul.

"You're Owen Patrick's daughter." A statement not a question. "Not exactly the young lady I'd have expected. Maybe you take after your mother."

Ellen felt a surge of hot Irish temper; that she definitely got from her father. Her mother had died when she was very young, and Ellen had few memories of her. But her father, grandparents, and friends of her parents had told her stories about her mother. Ellen might not remember much about her mother, but she knew the woman who gave birth to her. For this politician to imply that her mother was less than a perfect lady was almost too much. The anger clouded her thoughts. This weasel of a politician, a member of the political machine of California which stole her father away from her, had no right to even mention her mother.

Ellen was sorely tempted to ball up a fist and pop Sanford in the kisser but the calmer analytical part of her brain, told her to stop. Sanford was watching her like a hawk, for whatever reason he was testing her and she nearly fell into his trap.

Ellen smiled her brightest smile and let loose a peal of musical laughter. "Daddy always said that I was lucky I looked like my mother and not him."

"Ah yes, I knew your mother at school. She was a junior when I was a senior and she was as enchanting as you."

"I bet you call all the girls enchanting."

"I did when I asked your mother to the senior prom. She turned me down." There was an edge of bitterness to his voice.

Ellen decided to change the subject. "Now Mr. Sanford, what brings you over here to my good friend, Emilio's house? There's no election this year."

Ellen found that most men looked at her blonde hair, athletic physique and her feminine curves and assumed that she was a silly blonde bimbo suited only to hang off the arm of a man and incapable of an intelligent thought. Of course, Ellen did little to dissuade this impression and in many cases cultivated it.

Sanford looked disapproving at her through the pince-nez glasses perched on the bridge of his nose. "I heard that Mr. Romani had a run in with the law. I thought it was the neighborly thing to do."

Ellen's keen brown eyes swept over the man. With his pious demeanor and public statements on movie people, the last thing John Sanford would do was just drop over to check on the welfare of his movie star neighbor.

"Why that's the very reason that I came over too. The poor dear. I was going to cook him some dinner."

"Well, he seems to be in good hands. Let him know that I dropped by and that he is most welcome to come over and visit. We'll play a rousing game of chess or dominos."

"I'll see how Emilio feels after dinner, he might come over," Ellen said, her face betraying none of the wash of emotions flooding over her.

"My son, Samuel, has just learnt how to play and he's beating me already. I'm sure he'll be a chess master one day." Sanford lit up with paternal pride. "He'd like a new challenge. Although I suspect your game is dominos." The politician put emphasis on the last word and watched her reaction.

Owen Patrick taught his daughter to play both games as well as poker and, more importantly, the value of a good poker face. This talent was especially helpful in her exploits as the Domino Lady, and it proved its use here. Did Sanford suspect that she was the Domino Lady?

"Oh, my father and I used to play chess, but I could never beat him. I haven't played since he died."

Was it just Ellen's imagination but did a look of discomfort come over the politician's face when she mentioned her father's death? While Sanford was a part of the California political machine, it seemed too unlikely that he had any knowledge of her father's death, let alone any direct involvement.

"Um, I should head home. Lovely to meet you," Sanford stated as he spun on his heel and nearly ran down the driveway.

Ellen's brown eyes narrowed. Councilman Sanford would certainly bear further scrutiny after she finished helping Emilio. It could just be that Sanford was uncomfortable talking about death, Ellen had met people like that before, but her instincts told her that Sanford was hiding something. As the politician left the property, Ellen fished the key she had borrowed earlier out of her handbag. She unlocked the door and walked into the living room. Emilio was still there under the blanket where she left him. A gentle snore escaped his lips, telling Ellen that the drugs had worn off and he was sleeping naturally. Ellen left him to sleep; in his state he needed the rest. She kicked off her heels and felt the thick carpet pile under her feet.

Her stomach gave a little growl, in all the excitement she hadn't eaten since breakfast. Ellen made her way to the kitchen to try and rustle up something to eat. Sadly, the pantry hadn't magically restocked itself while she had been away. Had she planned ahead, she might have bought some groceries to make something.

She was about to give up and make herself a sandwich, when she spotted a can hiding in the back. Tomato Soup, the label announced proudly. "*Mmm, mmm, good,*" thought Ellen as she emptied the can into a saucepan and mixed in some water. She placed the pan onto the electric element and stirred the pot with a wooden spoon she'd found in a drawer.

She popped the toast in the toaster. Ellen was impressed with the pop-up toaster, she kept burning her own toast forgetting to turn it over. She might just have to get one for herself, she thought as she buttered the toast.

Ellen sensed someone behind her and spun around slashing out with the table knife. Emilio stared at her in horror as the blunt knife stopped just inches from his eyes. "I'm so sorry Emilio, you startled me."

"I thought I could help." The movie star retreated from the blade and collapsed into a kitchen chair. The actor looked dejected.

Ellen served up the soup. "C'mon now, you've have a bad day so you're hardly at your best."

Emilio blew on a spoonful of soup before eating it. "I usually come off better."

"While you slept I heard from Stevenson, he's offered to pay for the Johnny the Fixer. In fact, I have the money right here….." Ellen took the money from her bag and dropped it on the table as she stopped talking and cocked her head.

Emilio was about to eat a spoonful of soup and paused. Panic crossed his face.

The sound she heard did not repeat. "I must be imagining things," Ellen said laughing. "Now let me go powder my nose."

Emilio tucked into his soup; if he noticed that Ellen had taken her handbag he thought nothing of it. Ellen raced to the nearest room and quick changed again to the Domino Lady. If there was a problem, Domino Lady was better equipped than Ellen Patrick to handle it without too many questions. If she handled it right, it might even make Emilio look good in the press.

Ellen hung her dress on the hook on the back of the bathroom door and pulled on her slinky white dress that hugged all of her curves and wrapped her black cloak around her shoulders. Her brown eyes peered through the mask, Ellen became the young avenger. As she walked out the bathroom she saw a display on the wall that gave her an idea. She returned her trusty automatic to the concealed holster on her garter belt and pulled down one of the crossed sabers, a memento from the grand sword fight from The Gypsy. Domino Lady slipped out the side door of the house.

Domino Lady stood in the darkness allowing her eyes to adjust. She moved through the night like a panther on the prowl. The black cape effectively hid her from sight. To her left came the snap of a dry twig. This may simply be an animal wandering through but the following muffled curse soon eliminated that option.

The Domino Lady moved to her left and saw the figure of a larger man. Her lithe frame soon ate the distance between them. If the big man sensed her presence he gave no sign before the blade flashed out and sliced open the back of his hand.

The curses were not muttered any longer as the pain caused the intruder to release his gun. The weapon raced the flow of blood to the ground. But before either could hit, Domino Lady had retreated into the darkness.

The cries of pain brought the other intruders to the side of their companion. Grasping his injured hand, the man quickly told the others that he had been attacked. Domino Lady recognized the voice of Anderson the leader of the Trident. The other two shapes would then be Mulhoon and Schulz.

Anderson growled instructions for his partners to find Romani, whom he incorrectly assumed to be his attacker. Domino Lady stood hidden in the shadows of the large oak tree beside the house and as one of the un-injured cops came to towards her. With a deft sweep, she knocked off the man's hat revealing the bullet head of Schulz. The German swore and bent over to collect his missing headwear. The crooked cop exposed his derriere to the young avenger and co-opting Romani's comedic fighting style brought the flat of the blade across his buttocks. The big cop howled in a mix of pain and surprise. The big cop balled his fist and swung for the place where his attacker had been. Sadly, Domino Lady had drifted silently into the night once again and his fist slammed into the tree trunk. Had the blow connected with the Domino Lady it may have crushed her skull into pulp. That force sunk into solid oak and broke all four of the German's fingers.

Mulhoon heard his companion's cries of pain. The Irish born police officer made the sign of the cross to ward off evil. His attendance to Mass had been sporadic over the last few years and his belief almost nonexistent. In the daylight, Mulhoon would coolly laugh off the idea of the divine and other supernatural beasties. But here now in the dark he wasn't so sure.

The screams of pain from two of the toughest men he knew, put Mulhoon's nerves on edge. And what he saw as he turned to aid his companions did nothing to help. It was only a flash of long blonde hair but it was enough to call to mind the stories his Granny told of the banshee, the women who screamed to signal the upcoming demise in the family. Then Mulhoon remembered reading that Romani was a Gypsy. The travelers put curses on people like the evil eye. Romani had been looking at them all funny when they had him in the police station. The Irish cop gripped his gun a little tighter.

A sharp blade pressed against his throat and he choked back the scream of terror. So intent was he on the blade on the front of his neck that he never noticed the needle entering the back. The sedative kicked in and the big man collapsed drawing the sharpened blade across his throat.

The other two police officers heard the Irishman hit the ground and temporarily forgot their injured hands. Anderson had stemmed most of his bleeding with his tie. Schulz was so angry that Anderson could almost see him radiating red hot rage in the dark.

The big German had lost his gun during his altercation and snarling he pulled his pocket knife. He would cheerfully gut the actor who had embarrassed him, regardless of what Johnny said.

Anderson tripped over Mulhoon's unconscious body as he tried catch his partner. A few choice Swedish phrases escaped his lips as he dug into his pocket for the penlight he kept there. The first thing he saw was blood. "Schulz!" He called to his companion.

The burly German officer heard the concern in his leader's voice and put aside his vendetta for the moment. He followed the small pool of light from the torch to see his friend bleeding profusely from a slit throat. Anderson was trying to stop the blood with a rolled-up handkerchief. "Mein Gott, the actor got Mulhoon?"

"It looks that way," Anderson said. "I need you to get him to the doctor. I can handle the actor alone." The Swede put more confidence in his voice than he felt.

"But what he did to Mulhoon…" Schulz argued.

"Once he's treated you can come back and help me," Anderson commanded. "The actor ain't the only one who can whoop Hooligan Mulhoon."

It was true, Anderson had managed to knock out both of his subordinates at one time or another during the time they worked together. Schulz wasn't happy about the situation but as concern for his friend had taken the edge off of his blinding rage, he could see that this was best way to handle the situation. The bullet-headed police officer nodded his agreement and handed over his knife. "It might come in handy." He growled over his shoulder as he stooped to pick up the Irishman.

As soon as his men were clear, Anderson switched off the torch and waited for his night vision to return. The small weight of the knife in his hand felt good and gave him some comfort. He was ready for the actor to attack.

Or so he thought. Domino Lady had dropped the sword and taken to using some of her other weapons. One of the more unusual tools was her cape. During a trip to New York, a fellow crimefighter had taught her a baritsu move that effectively turned her cape into a whip. It was this move, she employed against the lone crooked cop.

The cape wrapped around his wrist and caused him to lose his grip on the knife. The big Swede reacted quickly and managed to grab hold of her cape. With a violent yank, he pulled on the material pulling the siren of justice off of her feet. She fell at his feet and felt the fallen pocket knife under her hand.

Thinking quickly the young adventuress palmed the blade and tucked it into her garter as she began to roll. Anderson's size twelve hoofers stomped the ground where her head had been a fraction of a second earlier. Her free hand reached for the clasp that held the cape around her neck. Anderson's grip on the cape was making it hard to open. The Domino Lady dived at the dirty cop; this gave enough slack to release the cape. The now open clasp flew from her neck and flicked in the face of Anderson. The metal hit him hard enough to break the skin and start the flow of blood.

The big Swede flailed in pain and his knee struck Domino Lady right in her solar plexus. Air whooshed from the debutante detective and she fell to the ground gasping for air.

Anderson smiled a cruel smile as his boot lashed out connecting with Domino Lady's head. As she drifted into the arms of Morpheus, Ellen found herself wondering how she would cover the mark that was going to leave.

The Domino Lady returned to the land of the living, a car engine roaring in her ear. Her head throbbed in time to the sound of passing traffic. She tried to move her hands and feet but she found them handcuffed. Anderson must have used his cuffs on her arms and when Schulz returned they put on the leg irons. The Domino Lady opened her eyes just a slit and could only see the roof of the car when the streetlights flashed into the window.

The car stopped and rose when one of the officers hopped out. The car idled for several minutes as Domino Lady tried to clear her head. The car again sunk before the door slammed shut.

Anderson addressed his colleague, "Johnny is going to meet us at the mill to collect the money we got from Romani. Those Hollywood types are just soft poseurs, he was at the door with the money before I even knocked. I'm a bit disappointed; I wanted the chance to rough up that pretty smile."

A truck roared past and Domino Lady missed the German's reply but the nasty laugh afterwards was enough to turn her blood into ice water. The drive continued with the flow of traffic becoming less and less the further they drove. Eventually, the car turned off what Domino Lady presumed to be the main road. The journey was relatively silent excluding the engine roar as the car hugged curves throwing the bound passenger around the floor of the car.

Schulz looked over into the back seat and saw the Domino Lady was awake. Next thing she saw was the German's giant mitt coming towards her. He was holding a white pad and the sickly-sweet smell of chloroform

"She fell at his feet..."

wafted into her nose. Domino Lady tried to hold her breath but it was too late she could already feel her consciousness slipping away for a second time.

When Domino Lady awoke for the second time, she had a throbbing headache. A quick check showed that there were no other injuries but that she had been bound to a log with the rope wrapped around her torso multiple times down to her knees. The heroine tested her bonds and found there was no give in the ropes. The Domino Lady raised her head and saw the log extended about three feet beyond the heels of her shoes.

"Ah! Sleeping Beauty awakes," came the familiar gravelly voice of Johnny. "Mr. Stevenson was kind enough to lend us his set. Not that we gave him much of a choice."

The slimy producer came into Domino Lady's field of vision. He had a smirk on his face that she just wanted to slap off which was not possible as her hands were bound by her side. Stevenson was brave when she was safely bound.

The Domino Lady had seen a number of the cliffhanger serials to know what was coming next. In the serials, the saw would start, the damsel would scream. The dashing hero would change in and save her. But this wasn't a serial and there was no dashing hero, only an actor who played one in the movies, Romani was probably curled up in the corner. So, if any escape was to happen, she'd have to save herself.

The buzz saw started behind the Domino Lady. Her hand touched her thigh and the knife she stashed in her garter. Either they hadn't searched her or missed the knife in their search. The log started moving towards the saw. Assuming that she had been tied in the middle of the log, there were three feet before she got a splitting headache. Her fingers painstakingly pulled out the knife and she pressed the button and the blade flew out.

The point slashed across her skin and caught the top of the stocking. Domino Lady was slightly annoyed at the loss of her stocking but at least it went for a good cause.

The Domino Lady gripped the handle and began to cut through the rope. The saw whined as its teeth bit into the hard timber of the log spurring her to cut faster. The sound of her captors' laughter rose over the noise of the saw as she struggled against her bonds.

The rope must have been nearly an inch thick but felt more like a foot as Domino Lady cut through the rope. The position was awkward and her hand began to cramp. With each movement she could feel the blade losing its edge. She briefly considered trying to turn over the knife and using the other edge but changing her grip was risking dropping the knife. She persisted with the knife, frantically cutting. The saw continued through the log and Domino Lady felt the wind from the blade begin to tug on her hair.

The cramping in her hand became more painful as she pushed the knife deeper into the rope. The fibers of the rope gave way under the pressure of the blade. She twisted her hips against the ropes. Just as she felt the splinters flung out by the circular saw hit the top of her blonde head, the rope finally parted and Domino Lady was free. The rope fell off of her body as she sat up, just before the circular saw put a new part in her hair.

The four men in attendance stood in stunned silence. It appeared Domino Lady was a ghost as the ropes seemed to melt off of her. This illusion was aided by the white dress blending with her porcelain skin. In the second it took the men to snap out of their stupor, the Domino Lady was already in action. Her left leg snapped out and landed a bone jarring kick to the jaw of Stevenson. His teeth snapped together, biting off the tip of his gilded tongue that had talked so many women onto his casting couch. The pain of that combined with the broken jaw caused the producer to fall unconscious.

The Domino Lady's right hand snapped out and returned the borrowed knife to the person she thought was its owner. Anderson jerked his head to one side and the blade buried itself in his left bicep. The same arm that had just drawn his pistol. Nerveless fingers fumbled with the gun and it landed barrel first on the ground.

The big cop dived for his weapon with his right hand and he pulled the trigger. This was a mistake. The blocked barrel caused the weapon to explode in his hand and shrapnel buried itself in his head, tearing off his right earlobe.

A stray piece of shrapnel whizzed in front of Schulz's eyes, causing him to flinch just as he fired at Domino Lady. The bullet flew out of the gun missing its intended target. The German detective looked over at his injured chief. The blonde hair was streaked red with blood. Over the years Schulz had come to believe that Anderson was nigh on invincible, the type of Aryan Ubermensch that Herr Hitler had said would rule the world. Schulz stared in disbelief at his fallen hero as the gun dropped from his hand.

This gave Domino Lady the opportunity to cross the distance between them and drive her last syringe of knockout drug into the big German. The man roared in pain as his good hand wrapped around the slim, pale throat of Domino Lady. His hand was so large that it almost wrapped around the vigilante's neck.

"Witch!" he roared as the drug raced through his adrenaline-charged system. His grip tightened momentarily before the strength slipped from his fingers. This was soon followed by a weakness in his legs as he dropped to the ground. The last thing Schulz felt was his bullet shaped head hitting the rock-hard dirt floor of the sawmill. The last thought through his head as consciousness slipped away was that he was going to have one hell of a headache.

The Domino Lady took a deep breath as the German's thumb slipped away from her trachea. She reached for his gun and found that like Anderson's the barrel had been jammed. The Domino Lady was completely unarmed as she turned and looked for Johnny.

The final conspirator was rapidly fleeing the scene. He hadn't lasted as long as he had without being able to read a situation and knowing when it was lost. Stories he'd heard whispered through the halls of power in California came back to him. Domino Lady had cut a swath through the corrupt in this state. Johnny had disbelieved the stories he'd heard about the Domino Lady. Nobody, let alone a woman, could destroy large criminal undertakings like The Black Legion alone. It was too impossible a notion to even give credit to, like some crazy tale from a pulp magazine. Yet the impossible had happened right before his very eyes as the Domino Lady took down two battle-hardened tough cops who broke up bar fights just for fun. This was after she had hospitalized the third member of his team of cops.

Johnny decided then and there that this was the time to get out of fixing things for Hollywood studios. He had fifty thousand dollars in the bag in his hand and at least two million stashed in accounts around the country. That was enough money to quietly live on as the heat died down.

He threw the bag in the back seat of his car and drove away from the sawmill. His eyes were glued to the rearview mirror but no cars were following him. He took a circular, roundabout route back to his house. The further he drove the less worried he became. Nobody knew Johnny's true identity and a few months from now he could start again with a new identity and a new disguise. The fake beard had served him well in this exploit so another disguise would be sure to work again. Hollywood was too lucrative to give up on entirely.

Certain that he was home free and that no one was following him, the man known as Johnny returned to his home. He turned the car into the driveway and was looking forward to removing the fake beard and seeing his family. To his surprise there was already a car in his garage. A police car. The car that the police unit known as the Trident drove. The car that had been at the sawmill.

Standing beside the car was a sight he did not want to see. A masked blonde woman in a ripped and torn white gown that did little to cover her voluptuous figure. She appeared to carrying a shotgun. The Domino Lady had come straight here. She was aware of his true identity. Johnny's mind raced, he could get out of this. He pulled up behind the police car and stepped out of the car, carrying the money bag. He looked Domino Lady right in the eyes.

"I have no idea how you knew was I coming to get the final payment from Councilman Sanford but I applaud your detective work." Johnny said in his gravelly voice.

Domino Lady smiled, "Oh Johnny, I suspected that you were Councilman Sanford for some time now. You just confirmed it."

The councilman nodded as he reached up with his free hand and pulled off the fake beard. "As a gambit, it was unsuccessful and that you appear to have me in check. May I pull my glasses from my pocket?"

Domino Lady aimed the Winchester Model 12 Shotgun directly at his chest and nodded. "You may also carefully remove the little pistol you carry, a Derringer I presume, and throw it on the ground. Checkmate."

If the Councilman was disappointed that his final gambit had been unsuccessful, he wasn't showing it. He reached into his coat and carefully removed his pistol and tossed it on the ground. He then pulled out his pince-nez and perched them on his nose. "Not that I really need the glasses, I find they lend me the air of old world trustworthiness for the voters. I am impressed trained police met me multiple times in both identities and never suspected they were the same man. You hear my voice a couple of times and you ferret out my deepest secret."

Domino Lady laughed. "Oh, I've been watching Councilman Sanford for some time now. You seem to be on the periphery of a number of shady deals and I was planning on paying you a midnight visit looking for proof of your corruption. It was just serendipity that I crossed paths with Johnny first."

The politician snarled, "I only take from those bloated Hollywood leeches sucking the money and morals from decent people. That gypsy next door, he seduced my 16-year-old niece and I swore that he would pay. I think he's paid quite handsomely."

With that the corrupt politician laughed. "It seems that we are not quite at checkmate but rather a stalemate. When you let me remove my disguise you gave away the leverage and proof that I was Johnny. You cannot prove a single allegation in a court of law. Costumed types cannot testify in court."

"I could kill you as you stand," Domino Lady threatened.

"Yet unlike some of your fellow vigilantes, you don't kill. I would already be dead if The Spider was standing before me. I've thought several moves ahead of you."

Domino Lady considered her next move, when a young boy ran out of the house. Like his father he had dark curly hair.

"Father, you're home!" the boy called as he jumped and hugged his father. "Let's play chess."

Domino Lady couldn't take down the man in front of his child. She retreated into the shadows of the garage as Sanford led his son into the house. Once the pair went inside, the Domino Lady retreated back to Emilio Romani's house.

She snuck back into the house and into the bathroom. Ellen removed the tatters of her dress and put her red sundress back on. She reapplied her make-up and tried to cover up the bruises on her head and throat. Ellen Patrick came out of the washroom looking a little worse for wear but still stunning. The make-up had covered all the visible injuries she had sustained.

Ellen found Romani curled up on the couch sleeping. The young woman shook him awake. "I just wanted to thank you for fighting off those men."

Confusion showed in the actor's eyes.

Ellen continued her lie. "You heard a noise and snatched the sword off the wall and went outside. I watched through the windows. It was like watching one of your movies; you even whacked one on the butt with the flat of your blade like you did in The Gypsy. In a brilliant stroke you knocked out another and made it look like you had slit his throat. You then parlayed with their leader and gave the money after the other two left for the hospital." Ellen made her voice almost giggly and excited. She touched his shoulder and flirted outrageously.

Emilio Romani was not immune to flattery and after several minutes had convinced himself that he had indeed fought the Trident to a standstill. He actually embellished the story with a few details liberally borrowed from his movies. By the time the story made the papers Romani had single handedly vanquished a dozen men. Romani was due to star in the movie version produced by a very tight-lipped Harold Stevenson.

Ellen was happy for the actor to get all the credit, just as a discreet call to Paul Cathern gave the special deputy the arrest of the Trident. The three were happy to talk; it appeared that Sanford's disguise was not as fool proof as he thought as all three sang like canaries.

With the new information the police dropped all charges against Romani. The actor was so grateful that he invited Ellen, J.C. Moore and his wife Lacey to lunch. Ellen drove the married couple to the lunch and her raven-haired friend chattered the entire way about how excited she was to finally meet her screen idol.

Ellen nearly didn't recognize the Emilio Romani that opened the door to greet them. Gone was the tension and haggardness. He was immaculately dressed and seemed to have gotten nearly a decade younger. Lacey blushed as he flashed his million-dollar smile at her during the introductions. She nearly swooned when he kissed her hand and in his Gypsy accent vowed to fight her husband for her heart, it was a line from The Gypsy.

Emilio laughed and returned to his natural voice. "I find the fans love that line, the husbands not so much." The smile returned and even Ellen was starting to feel its effects.

J.C. laughed at his client's joke and put up his fists. "I'm no Battling Battalino but I'm willing to put up a fight."

The darkly handsome actor laughed and threw up his hands. "I surrender."

"I start training next month to play the undisputed champion Barney Ross in a movie." He stage-whispered to the ladies with an exaggerated wink. "After that all bets are off."

Ellen and Lacey laughed as their host led them through the house and onto the verandah. The outdoor table had been set with fine China and silver cutlery. "Ellen, you'll find a larger range of food than your last visit." He said as he pulled out her chair. The blonde socialite noticed that the seat gave her an excellent view of Sanford's house.

The quartet sat and enjoyed their meal with much laughter and frivolity. After the plates had been cleared by the waiter, Emilio offered some Canadian iced tea.

It was then that Ellen noticed several cars pull up at the Sanford house and the familiar figure of Paul Cathern made his way to the house. The other police milled around as Cathern pounded on the door.

Lacey enquired as to what had taken her attention from their very handsome and eligible host and the party watched the rest of the raid. Losing patience, Cathern slammed one of his police issue boots into the front door of the house. It must have been her imagination but Ellen would have sworn that she heard the cracking of the doorframe. The half dozen cops followed their leader into the house and nearly thirty minutes later all the police came out empty handed.

"I saw Sanford and his family drive off last night." Romani said as he sipped the Canadian brew from the teacup. "I was having trouble sleeping, worried about the charges and the car flew out of the driveway. I swore that he was going to hit the mailbox down the street. I'm surprised that he didn't leave big skid marks the way he was driving. "

The party spent a lovely afternoon together after that and Ellen and J.C. nearly had to drag Lacey to the car. Ellen dropped the couple off and drove back to her apartment. She was determined to get the full story from Cathern.

Ellen unlocked the door to find that the phone was already ringing. She raced across the room to find that Cathern had the same idea. The Special Deputy confirmed that Sanford and his family had fled. A warrant had been issued for John Sanford's arrest but there were no leads.

It was nearly a year later that Ellen Patrick was invited to the premiere of Romani's Gangbuster in the nearby coastal Palm City. The party was crowded, yet Ellen swore for the briefest of instants that she had seen a very familiar face. The glasses were gone, the hair had been straightened and slicked back and the man had been sporting a moustache that might have made Clark Gable cry but it was definitely the face of disgraced councilor John Sanford.

The socialite was due to return to Hollywood but she had to track down this man, if she was not mistaken this was the first real lead on the elusive mastermind of the Hollywood extortion ring. Her companion that evening was over-joyed that Ellen had decided to stay longer. Asking discreetly, Ellen discovered that no one knew who this mystery man was and that he had disappeared from the premiere.

The next morning, Ellen began her investigation in earnest. While she was prepared to spend hours poring over musty old papers in the local library, there was an easier way. Sanford had a son, Samuel. The boy looked about ten when she saw him that night a year ago and Palm City only had three schools that taught eleven-year olds. Two elementary and one junior high school.

It was the second school, Palm City Elementary, where Ellen struck gold. She had spun a yarn about her father bequeathing some money to his godson, who she didn't know about until the reading of the will. The old man had hand written the will and while they couldn't make out the surname but thought the first name might be Samuel. Luckily not only was there only one Samuel in the age range and the school had just released their yearbook and Ellen was not only able to look at a photo but confirm that the boy was a member of the chess team. The lady in the office even gave her the name of the boy, Samuel Fleming, and his address in the swankier areas of Palm City.

Now that Ellen had an address and surname it was a simple matter of looking through some public records in the Town Hall to find out more about the newly minted James Fleming. Fleming was the founder and CEO of Ark Investments. The plans for his house were on file there as well. Ellen spent the afternoon taking notes and figuring how the Domino Lady might best pay her old enemy a visit.

That night Ellen made excuses to her host and drove her car across town and in a secluded glade slipped out of her dress and into the skin-tight, nearly sheer, white dress that left little to the imagination. She then covered her kissable shoulders with a deep black cape. Her eyes were masked with the black domino mask. The outfit was accessorized with her trusty pistol, several knockout syringes and a lockpick set.

The Domino Lady slipped through the night to the back door of the Fleming mansion. The lock succumbed to her lockpicks in a matter of seconds and she slipped into the house. The light of her penlight led her through the lower floor of the house to the room indicated as study on the plans and she went straight to the area marked as a built-in safe on the same plan. The picture swung out on oiled hinges and Domino Lady was soon looking at a very new Graylock safe. Her fingers twirled the dials as she listened for the tell-tale clicks, with one ear listening for sounds in the house. The safe opened and Domino Lady found several piles of cash.

The seductive avenger looked for something to carry the money and found a bag sitting beside the desk, in a moment of realization Domino Lady recognized the bag was same one that John Sanford had used to carry the money he had extorted from Emilio Romani. It seemed appropriate to use it to retrieve those funds. The Domino Lady took the all the money from the safe, after all he had merely borrowed the fifty thousand and the interest was due. The young avenger placed one of her trademark black cards in the now empty safe.

The next morning the man now known as James Fleming went to his study to read the stock market prices on his ticker tape machine and found the safe door open. He swore long and loudly as he read the white writing that said: COMPLIMENTS OF THE DOMINO LADY.

The End

Behind the Scenes
The Domino Lady's Scandal

*W*hen I was writing my first Domino Lady story Domino Lady's Triple Threat, I reread the six Lars Anderson stories and I noticed that Anderson didn't seem to utilise the Hollywood setting as much as he could have. It may have been the plan for the next batch of stories or maybe it was the domain of Spicy/Saucy Hollywood stories.

I was already committed to a different story for that story but the idea of a more Hollywood story bubbled away in the back of my brain. Then I read Errol Flynn's My Wicked, Wicked Ways where Flynn talks about an anonymous voice extorting him over the phone before his arrest for statutory rape. This seemed like a good scandal for The Domino Lady.

But this was several years after the end of the stories so I looked at earlier actors and played with the Latin Lover actors like Rudolf Valentino and Ramon Navarro, .

I created Emilio Romani, the man with the million-dollar smile, star of The Gypsy, Son of the Gypsy and others. Many of Romani's views are much the same as Errol Flynn, especially in regards to rape, the story of Romani finding a naked girl in bed was also borrowed from Flynn.

I knew when I started writing that there would be a skeevy producer filming his exploits on the casting couch. In the middle of writing the story, the Harvey Weinstein story broke, Art imitating life imitating art, I did briefly consider taking Stevenson out but I enjoyed writing a character with whom The Domino Lady had some history.

I mentioned the pulp character "Satan" Devlin several times in this story. In Bernard A. Drew's introduction to The Domino Lady: The Complete Collection, it was mentioned that Lars Anderson was the author of the Satan Devlin stories. At the start of this project I considered giving Satan Devlin a role, teaming up two of Lars Anderson's creations, but it was nearly impossible to find any information about the character. I later discovered that Ernst Manning wrote the stories not Lars Anderson. I did however litter the story with references to other pulp characters both classic and new.

This was the first time I had written a second story for the same character and it was nice to revisit an old friend. I hope you enjoy revisiting her with me.

BRAD MENGEL - works in Australia's criminal justice system. Before that he was trolley boy, a barman, an office manager and a teacher. A lifelong reader and pulp fan it was natural that he would turn to writing. His book *Serial Vigilantes of Paperback Fiction: An Encyclopedia from Able Team to Z-Comm* (McFarland, 2009) was the first book to examine vigilante fiction of the 70s and 80s. He has also contributed stories to Tales of *The Shadowmen* #3 & #7, *Pro Se Presents* Nov 2012, *Charles Boeckman Presents Johnny Nickle, Pulp Obscura: Senorita Scorpion* and *Blood & Tacos* #4 and *The Destroyer: More Blood*. His series *Australis Incognito* is coming soon from Pro Se.

OPEN GRAVE

By Gene Moyers

The Domino Lady wheeled her car carefully up winding Fern Dell Drive in the hills above Hollywood. She drove without headlights; the only illumination on the dark road the bright moonlight that bathed the road in soft light. She entered a long switch back that gave her a spectacular view of the glittering lights of Los Angeles below and to her right. On this open stretch she braked slightly to let the car she was following draw ahead. Soon that car passed into the darker shadows of a tree lined bit of road and the masked woman pressed the accelerator down to close up a bit on the big Plymouth sedan.

She had followed the car and it's occupants up from Hollywood. First on Wilshire, then up Western to Los Feliz and finally onto Fern Dell that wound up Mt. Hollywood into Griffith Park. There were four men in the Plymouth; three tough hoods and a captive that the Domino Lady was intent on rescuing.

The Domino Lady's alter ego, Ellen Patrick was dating a handsome young movie star who had signed with Paramount Studios. Through him she had heard rumors of trouble in the studio production industries. Ellen had snooped around and found that someone was attempting to muscle in on the various industries that supported the movie studios; industries such as electricians, catering, transportation and the like. Since the death of her father at the hands of a corrupt political machine, Ellen had devoted her life to rooting out corruption in her beloved 'Golden State' and this certainly fell into that category. Tonight the Domino Lady had been watching a group of hoods that were involved in this racket attempting to find out who was behind them. She had been surprised when they had met a man who they beat up and threw in the back of their car.

She was now behind that car wondering where they were going and fearing the worst. Just before they reached the tunnel running through the hills where the road turned into Vermont Canyon Drive, she saw the Plymouth's brake lights flash as the car slowed. It turned off to the right and disappeared through the trees. Reaching the turn off spot she found a dirt road next to a large sign announcing the construction company that was building the new Griffith Park Observatory.

She knew that ground had recently been broken for the new observatory and major work was proceeding. She turned off and slowly followed the winding road. When she saw lights through the trees, she turned off to the left and found a place to park amongst a clump of trees. Outside on foot she moved slowly through the trees toward the lights. Along the way she stopped and reached up under her long black dress to pull her small automatic pistol from its holster.

Reaching the edge of the trees she peered out. The large open area in front of her had been cleared of trees and underbrush. Fresh dirt plowed flat, spread out for over a hundred yards in all directions. Tall wooden stakes with white ribbons tied to them marked off large and small plots. Twenty five yards away five men stood in a rough circle illuminated by the headlights of two automobiles. A sixth man was on his knees in the midst of them. The masked woman gripped her pistol harder. The men she had been following had met two more already here. This changed things. Now the odds were five to one and she was painfully aware that her little pistol held only six rounds.

The man on the ground was loudly pleading for his life. The Domino Lady's mind raced as she searched desperately for a way to save the man. Perhaps some kind of distraction would help. As she looked for inspiration, one of the men stepped forward and swung his revolver at the man on the ground. Struck in the head the man flopped limply forward onto the ground. She could hear the gunman clearly as he shoved his gun back under his coat, "Okay, you two finish him off and bury him. Make it look good. When you're finished, drop your car at the warehouse." He thought for a moment before adding, "They'll be laying concrete in this area in a day or two. This guy will disappear forever." There were a couple of low laughs at this.

She watched as the leader and two others turned around and boarded the Plymouth she had followed. Relieved that there was still a chance to save the innocent captive, she watched as the Plymouth turned and made its way back the way it had come. Now the odds were more to her liking. Turning, Domino Lady saw the two remaining men dragging the unconscious man toward a pile of fresh dirt she had not noticed before. Undoubtedly these two had come here early to dig a grave. She reached under her dress and pulled out a capped syringe. She pulled off the cap with her teeth and spat it out. She then stepped out from the trees and walked as carefully as she could in her low heels toward the two men. She got close behind one of the men before she was seen by the other. He dropped his shovel and yelled, "Hey!" She quickly stepped forward and ground her pistol barrel into the ear of the nearest hood; "Alright, everybody freeze!" she called out.

The man across from her reached for a gun. She stopped him with a command, "Don't try it!" The hood she was holding whined, "Look lady you got the…" She cut him off, "Shut up! You! Drop your gun or your pal here gets it!" The second gunman hesitated for a moment then slowly brought his revolver out and dropped it at his feet. Keeping her pistol on the man in front of her she commanded, "Now raise your hands and turn around." The second man complied and she added, "Good. Now take a few steps backwards."

When he had done so, she told him, "Stop. Now stand very still." Domino Lady then swung her pistol hard against the hood's head in front of her. He collapsed to the ground limply. She took three quick steps forward and jabbed the second man in the neck with the syringe. He clapped a hand to his neck and yelled, "Owww!" before slumping to the ground unconscious from the quick acting drug she had injected him with.

Last woman standing; the Domino Lady moved quickly to the still form lying in the moonlight next to his intended grave. A quick examination confirmed that the man was unconscious but alive. She stood up and looked thoughtfully around. The man she had injected would be out for hours, but the man she had struck would probably be coming around in a few minutes. She glanced at the two unconscious mobsters and then at the open grave. A quick glance at her watch convinced her she would have to move quickly.

Frank "Buddy" Latimer woke up to a throbbing headache. He groaned and reached for his head but found he couldn't move his arm. In fact he couldn't move either arm. He blinked. His vision was slightly obscured and as he shook his head dirt flew from his face. This startled him wide awake. It was dark all around him with a narrow band of starry sky above him. Before his mind could catch up with events, a shovelful of dirt landed on his chest. He tried to call out but dirt that had landed on his face caught in his open mouth. He spit, spluttered aloud and coughed.

Panicky he squirmed attempting to sit up. He realized then that his hands were tied behind him as were his legs. He was lying on his hands looking up from an oval hole in the ground. Further there was a limp body crushed in next to him, laying half to one side and half on top of him.

Terrified he spat dirt and yelled, "Hey! Somebody Help!" just as more dirt landed on his legs. There was silence for a moment before a shadowy face leaned over the edge of the grave above him. He couldn't see the shadowy features but it looked like a woman with long hair looking down at him.

Domino Lady leaned on the shovel and looked at the mobster in the bottom of the grave. It had taken nearly ten minutes for him to come around from the blow on his head. During this time she had tied his hands and feet with cord she had found in the men's car. She had then rolled him and his unconscious partner into the grave. A few shovelfuls of dirt had completed the setting for her little drama. Looking down at the terrified man she observed calmly, "Oh, you're awake." She then dug her shovel into the pile of loose earth and tossed another shovelful onto his legs. He screamed out "Wait! What are you doing?" Confident that no one could hear his screams she called out confidently, "Getting rid of some vermin," as she added more dirt in on top of him.

Latimer could feel his bladder about to let go as he yelled, "You can't do this!"

Domino Lady replied, "Sure I can. You two just murdered an innocent man. This is what you deserve." Another shovelful of dirt followed the others. Latimer screamed out, "No! He's not dead! We didn't hurt him. Please!"

The masked woman stopped and leaned over the open grave, "You mean you didn't have time to kill him before I got here? What's his name?"

Latimer licked his dusty lips and whispered, "His name is Fredericks."

Squatting down at the edge of the hole she grabbed up a handful of dirt and trickled it over the man's chest, "I can't hear you."

"Fredericks! His name is Fredericks!"

"Why does he have to die?"

His chest heaving Latimer gasped out, "He wouldn't play ball. He was going to the police."

"Why is he so important?"

"He's the union rep for the electrician's local."

"And you were leaning on him. Muscling in on the union?"

Latimer was shivering and terrified but now sweat sprung out on the mobster's forehead. How could this woman know so much? Who was she?

"We were just…"

"Who gave the order?"

"What?"

"Your boss; the guy in the Plymouth. Who is he?"

Latimer licked his lips and hesitated. He hesitated a moment too long because another handful of dirt quickly landed on his face. He choked and gagged. Finally spitting out dirt he gasped, "Travis! His name is Travis."

Domino Lady frowned, "Is he calling the shots?"

"Whadda ya mean?"

"Is Travis the big guy behind all of this?"

"Uh, no."

"Then who is?'"

"We don't know?"

"Okay. I guess we're done." Latimer heard the shovel dig into the dirt pile and saw it silhouetted against the moonlit sky above him. He screamed out, "It's true! We don't know! Only Travis talks to him!"

Domino Lady thought for a moment, "The warehouse you're supposed to go to: where is it?"

Defeated Latimer spilled out, "It's off Fairfax."

"Where?" He quickly reeled off a West Hollywood address. Domino Lady stood up, "You two deserve a lot worse than this." She turned and walked away. As she reached the men's car; she pulled out her gun and fired a bullet into the front tire. It blew with a bang. She then reached into the front of her dress and pulled out a small card. The bright moonlight reflected off the white lettering on the black card. It read: *Compliments of the Domino Lady.* She placed the card under one of the windshield wipers on the car's windshield. As she did she could see the unconscious Fredericks lying on the front seat of the car where she had placed him. She turned and walked through the trees to where her coupe was hidden. As she reached her car she could hear the distant screams of her captive in the open grave.

Three minutes later she was pulling back onto the paved road. She immediately powered down the hill toward the city. She was a good driver and the road was empty this late at night. With her headlights on, she made good time. Five minutes later she was leaving the park and turning on to Los Feliz. Here there were more cars but it was late and traffic was still light. Soon she turned west onto Hollywood Blvd. When she reached Fairfax she began looking for the street the frightened thug had named.

Once she found it she turned off her headlights and drove slowly down the street looking for the correct address. She quickly located it. Sure enough it was a small warehouse with a large *For Lease* sign on the front wall. As she passed it Domino Lady recognized the Plymouth she had followed up to Griffith Park parked at the curb. She continued past and parked her coupe down the block.

Walking back to the warehouse she noted dim light coming from a series of high windows in the warehouse. She frowned for a moment wondering if there was another entrance. She really needed to know if all three of the mobsters or more were inside. She looked around. A narrow alley ran alongside the building. She entered it and waited for her eyes to adjust to the darkness. Soon she made out a battered metal garbage can a few yards away but no side door. She hefted the can; not very full. She carried it out onto the empty sidewalk and placed it under one of the windows, hiked up her long dress and climbed up onto the ill smelling can.

Standing on tip toes atop the garbage can she could just see over the sill into the dimly lit interior. The warehouse floor was mostly empty. Dominating the space was a long table. Several mismatched chairs sat around it. Papers and what looked like a map were scattered across it. An overflowing ashtray on the table was matched by an overflowing wastebasket next to it. A lone man sat at the table cleaning a revolver while smoked a cigarette. Most of the overhead lights were out leaving the far corners in darkness but he appeared to be alone.

Domino Lady climbed carefully down from the garbage can and looked around. The industrial street was still empty of movement. It looked like the other mobster's had left. Was this Travis? It had to be; he would be awaiting word from the two undertakers she had left up in Griffith Park. She smiled; if he was expecting company he wouldn't be surprised when someone showed up.

She slipped to the door. As she did she drew her pistol and another of her handy syringes that she had taken from the glove compartment of her car. She gently tried the knob. The knob turned but the door didn't budge; locked as she had suspected. Straightening she knocked loudly with the butt of her pistol. There was a quick noise then a sudden hush from inside. Immediately footsteps approached the door. A latch turned and as the door swung open a man's voice complained, "About time you guys showed up. I want to get home." The door swung fully open and the Domino Lady, her gun arm straight out shoved the muzzle of her little automatic into the face of the surprised man.

Travis, shocked by the appearance of a masked woman in a black dress, couldn't react before her pistol jammed painfully into his nose. Forced backward he instinctively reached for his gun but it was lying unloaded on the table. He raised his hands in front of him and yelled, "Hey take it ea…"

The masked woman cut him off, "Get those hands up!"

Confronted with a gun muzzle pressed against his nose, Travis gave ground and shot his hands upwards. He stopped when his backside hit the edge of the table. Trying to get control he spoke, "Look lady I don't know what…"

She again cut him off mid-sentence, "Do you know who I am?"

Travis finally managed to focus on the actual figure before him. He took in the long black dress, the long white cape and the Domino Mask. He had only heard talk and vague descriptions but he had no doubt that the masked figure who stood before him was the mysterious Domino Lady that the local underworld was talking about. Attempting to remain calm he nodded in answer to her question. She continued, "Then you know how much trouble you're in." Before he could answer this she added fiercely, "I just saw you order the death of an innocent man in Griffith Park so I'm not inclined to be patient or merciful. Understand?"

Travis went cold at her words. How could she know that? And where were Buddy and Jack? He had to stall until they got here. He cleared his throat, "You got the wrong man Domino Lady. I'm just the night watchman here waiting for my relief."

Her voice was cold as she spoke again, "Sure you are. Where's your uniform? I see your gun over there. Guess it got some blood on it when you smacked Fredericks in the face?"

Travis went pale. How could she know this stuff? He licked his dry lips, "Uh, no. No, you've made a…" She smiled coldly as she cut him off, "I suppose you're stalling, waiting for your two friends. Sorry, they won't be joining the party any time soon. I'm afraid I left them both in the grave they dug for Fredericks."

She let that one sink in as Travis went paler. She continued, "You're a kidnapper and a murderer. I won't have any trouble leaving you just like I left your two pals. Your only hope is to tell me what I want to know."

Travis could see the heat in her gaze. He nodded wordlessly. She spoke again, "I know you're in a racket trying to muscle in on the Hollywood trades. I don't think you're smart enough to be in charge. Tell me who's behind it?"

Licking his lips the frightened mobster whispered, "I don't know who he is."

The Domino Lady lifted her other hand high so that light glittered off the bare stainless steel needle. She leaned in slightly and said coolly, "This contains a drug that will kill you in seconds. It will seem like a heart attack to whoever finds you but I can tell you that your last few moments will be very painful. So talk now while you have the chance."

Travis could see no mercy in her face. Despite her obvious femininity this woman meant business. He capitulated, "Okay, I don't know his last name but there's a phone number where I can reach him."

"He doesn't have a name?" she asked suspiciously.

"He said to call him George."

"What else do you know about him?"

Travis hesitated and Domino Lady moved the needle closer to his throat. He quickly gasped out, "Okay! I think he's some big shot in the industry."

What industry?"

"Movies; Whadda ya think? I mean he knows everybody. We get all our info from him. Besides, who else'd wanna muscle in on these rackets?"

Domino Lady thought this over for a moment. It made sense. She asked Travis, "What's the number?"

With the little pistol's muzzle still pressed into his face Travis very carefully fished out his wallet. It took a moment of fumbling before he managed to find a folded piece of paper. His hand shaking he unfolded it and held it up. Sure enough, written there was a phone number under the name George.

Satisfied that she had found out what she came for the Domino Lady lifted the syringe so that Travis could see it and smiled, "Good bye Travis." She then plunged the needle into his neck injecting the knock out drug into his system. His eyes opened wide in momentary terror then closed as he passed out.

With the hood safely unconscious Domino Lady closed and locked the street door. She then quickly searched the place. The map turned out to be an L.A. street map with certain locations circled on it. Other papers were lists of names and businesses, union rosters and other information on the Hollywood trades. A nearby table held weapons and ammunition. There were also stacks of workmen's uniforms and coveralls; disguises, no doubt. She nodded grimly. The police would find all this very interesting. She just needed to attract their attention.

There was a phone on the wall. Lifting it she got a dial tone. She dialed 0 and waited. When the operator answered she asked for the police. In a few moments a male voice came on the line, "Police Department; Hollywood division."

Holding a fold of her cape across her mouth Domino Lady spoke slowly, "Listen carefully. There are two hoods waiting for you at Griffith Park where they're building the new observatory. They dragged a guy up there

She then plunged the needle into his neck…

to kill him. He's still alive but you better get up there right away... and take a doctor along. The rest of the gang is working out of a West Hollywood warehouse." She gave the address and continued before the startled policeman could interrupt her, "The leader is there now. He and his buddies are running a protection racket. You'll find plenty of evidence. Better get moving right away." She dropped the ear piece to dangle alongside the wall mounted phone. As it swung there she could hear a tinny voice yelling out, "Who is this? It better..." The voice cut off as Domino Lady fired her pistol into the wall near the phone. A shot fired ought to get them moving faster, she thought.

She left everything as it was and walked out of the warehouse leaving the outer door wide open. Minutes later she was heading east on Hollywood Blvd, her mask off and driving carefully when a squad car roared past her going in the opposite direction, siren blaring. She nodded. That was the second one she had passed. Now to get home and take a long bath.

Ellen Patrick was bored. She had been following her quarry most of the day and had seen nothing to help her. Worse she had been doing this a lot lately trying to get evidence on Douglas Roberts. Roberts was an ex-prosecutor from upstate. He had been turned out at the last election after suspicions that he had been accepting bribes for years from bootleggers and other organized crime members. Hard evidence against him had been lacking and he had not yet been prosecuted. Even the IRS had gotten involved looking for evidence of illegal income.

Since Roberts had not been disbarred he moved to LA and established a small legal practice. He didn't seem to have many clients but he certainly had lots of time to patronize nice restaurants and date attractive young starlets. Ellen was sure he had lots of ill-gotten money stashed somewhere but she couldn't seem to find it. Domino Lady had covertly searched both his apartment and his office and found nothing. If only she could find where his money was stashed she could sick the IRS on him, and once they were squeezing him anything could happen. She might even be able to get some money back to help in her favorite causes.

Now she was sitting outside the popular *Formosa* restaurant waiting for Roberts to finish his lunch. But she couldn't get last night's activities out of her mind. First thing this morning she had set out to find out "George's" identity. Her good friend Roger McKane was a detective employed by a well-known San Francisco agency. A while back he had shown her an interesting item known as a reverse directory. Printed by the phone company, it indexed phone numbers rather than names and gave the names and addresses assigned to a particular phone number. These useful books were normally only issued to public agencies such as police and fire departments. Fortunately Roge had helped her get one that covered the greater LA area. Locating the number she found it was issued to a *G. Monteaux* at a Hollywood Hills address. Could 'G' be for George?

She had called the number but no one had answered after many rings. The name had sounded familiar somehow but she had no time to puzzle it out. Hurriedly, she had dressed and headed out to spend her day following Roberts; hoping he might somehow lead her to his stash of money. At that moment her musings were interrupted as Roberts left the restaurant and crossed to his car. She reached for the starter on her roadster but then froze.

G. Monteaux! George Monteaux! Of course; the movie producer! Monteaux was well known in Hollywood circles as being a behind the scenes money man. He was an independent producer who had bankrolled many Hollywood hits. Ellen had heard that he had also bankrolled several recent flops as well. Could he be behind this new mob? Snapping out of her reverie Ellen started her car and hurried to catch up with Roberts.

She followed him back to his office and an hour later followed him home. After an hour of growing bored watching his apartment she shrugged in disgust, started her car and drove north. A half hour later she was driving through the Hollywood hills. Here many of the city's movers and shakers lived in large, fashionable homes. She had no trouble locating Monteaux's address. As she watched a brand new Auburn Boat Tail Speedster turned into Monteaux's long driveway. Was that the man himself? Ellen nodded. It looked like it was time to get to know George Monteaux better. She turned her car for home.

"Of course you'd be welcome Silly! George loves having pretty girls at his parties."

Ellen smiled. She had made a few calls and found a way to meet George Monteaux. Her friend Joanne was young starlet just breaking into

Hollywood. Her beauty and figure had got her a few small parts in movies and she was anxious to further her career. It turned out that Monteaux was having a party at his house this coming Saturday. Ellen had told her friend that a party sounded like fun and soon the young actress was urging Ellen to come along. Ellen tried to sound doubtful, "Are you sure? I'm not an actress. I'm just looking to meet a few new people."

"Silly, it's all the same thing."

"Okay then, I'll drive. What time should I pick you up?"

"How about eight?"

Ellen nodded, "I'll see you then." Goodbyes were spoken and Ellen hung up and smiled. She was looking forward to meeting this movie producer.

Saturday night Ellen picked up Joanne in plenty of time to drive to their destination. Monteaux's expensive home was in the Hollywood Hills with a fine of view of the city. It was a modern, split level building with a steel frame and concrete walls painted white and built on several levels. The entrance and multi-car garage was on the upper level and was approached by a long winding street along which were other million dollar homes.

The courtyard in front of the house was filled with parked cars, as was the long drive way. Ellen parked her roadster on the street at the top of the drive behind a Cord Cabriolet and the two girls walked down to the front door. Their knock was quickly answered by a formally dressed man servant and they were admitted with a small smile. Pretty girls were always welcome at a Hollywood party.

Past the entry way and wide hall was a large living room. More than a dozen well-dressed people were drinking and mingling there. A portable bar had been set up near the open doors leading outdoors.

Joanne squeezed Ellen's arm and whispered, "Oh, there's someone I know." She winked at Ellen and headed toward a small knot of people laughing and conversing. Ellen crossed to the bar. Prohibition had been repealed for the evening and she asked for champagne. Then glass in hand she walked through the wide doors onto the patio. Several couples strolled around the pool or stood on the bordering grass sipping drinks. It was a beautiful night. The moon had not yet risen and there were countless stars overhead. She admired the view of the city lights while she considered her approach to Monteaux.

Soon she re-entered the living room and looked for her friend. She didn't see Joanne and moved on. Across the hall she found her laughing at something her male companion was saying. As Ellen approached she turned and said, "Oh George, here's Ellen now." The tuxedo clad man turned and Ellen had her first close look at George Monteaux. He was of medium height and slim build. He had very dark hair swept back from his face and Gallic good looks. As Ellen held out her hand Joanne said, "George, this is Ellen Patrick. Ellen, George Monteaux." Monteaux bent and brushed his lips across the back of her hand and smiled, "It's a pleasure Miss Patrick. Joanne did not exaggerate your beauty."

Ellen smiled back. Oh, this one was a charmer, "Why thank you Mr. Monteaux, and please call me Ellen."

"If you call me George, you must be an actress as well?"

Ellen laughed, "No. I'm afraid not. I leave the acting to Joanne."

Monteaux feigned surprise, "Then that is the studios' loss. Perhaps you've done some modeling then?"

"No. I just enjoy going to parties."

Both girls laughed at this as Monteaux smiled. Ellen looked around and commented, "What a lovely home you have, George."

"Thank you Ellen. Would you care to see more?"

Joanne raised an eyebrow and said, "I'll go and find some more champagne." Monteaux offered his arm and Ellen took it as they walked down the hall. He showed her the lavishly appointed kitchen and dining room while stopping to exchange words with some of his guests. As they strolled, Ellen recognized a couple of major actors and several young girls she was sure she had seen in small movie parts.

As they passed a stairwell she pointed, "What's down there?"

"There is a music room, my study some guest bedrooms as well as another outdoor area."

Ellen squeezed his arm, "It sounds lovely. May I see it?"

"Of course." He led her down the stairs. To the left he then led her into a large open room which contained a grand piano. The second one she had seen Ellen thought. The room had a beautiful parquet floor that could easily be used for dancing. Laughter drew their attention and she followed Monteaux out onto a smaller, more intimate grass covered area with yet another wonderful view. Nearby a couple were in an intimate embrace in the shadows.

Ellen smiled at Monteaux as she whispered, "What a wonderful view." He took her hand and said, "Until Joanne returns perhaps you would like to have a drink in my study. I have a private bar there." And a couch, no doubt, thought Ellen as she allowed herself to be led back into the house. They left the music room and had just reached the door of Monteaux's study when Joanne bounced down the stairs with a glass in each hand. She looked excitedly at Monteaux, "George! Daryl Zanuck just arrived and is looking for you!"

Monteaux looked torn for a moment then looked regretfully at Ellen, "I'm sorry. Perhaps we can have that drink later. Please excuse me." He turned and hurried up the stairs. Joanne handed Ellen a glass and said, "Isn't it exciting. Daryl Zanuck is now head of production at Warner Brothers. I'm going to see if I can get an introduction." She too turned and hurried up the stairs leaving Ellen happily alone.

She quickly opened the door and stepped into Monteaux's study. This seemed the most likely place for him to keep his secrets. Inside she moved to his desk; fortunately it was unlocked. She searched through every drawer but found nothing out of the ordinary; normal correspondence, household bills, a checkbook and various memos and studio papers. She looked up. Across from her was a full wall of built in bookshelves. To her left were French doors leading out onto a small grassy area with a different view of the city. A table of bottles and glasses stood near it. There was also a sofa and a wing back chair and reading light near it.

She looked behind the three paintings on the walls for a concealed wall safe but again found nothing. Ellen chewed her lip lightly. A man like Monteaux must have a secure place to keep his money and anything he didn't want curious eyes to see. It might be in his bedroom. But before she began searching for his bedroom she decided to check the bookshelf for a hidden safe.

As she started around the desk, Ellen glanced down at the telephone. A small white card was slipped into a slot in the base of the handset. On it was a telephone number. It was not the number she had been given by Travis. She considered this; the reverse directory had showed that number registered at this address yet the house number was different. That's why no one had answered when she had called. There must be a private line somewhere in the house.

She moved to the bookshelf. It covered a complete wall; each vertical section was about four feet wide. As she began searching behind books, she thought about Monteaux's bedroom wondering if it was on this lower level. After a few minutes she was about to give up on the books when she felt one section of the bookshelves give slightly.

She leaned into it and definitely felt the far left section of shelves move slightly. She quickly moved her search to the far edge of the shelves and soon found a small section of wood that moved under her fingers. Pressing it resulted in a 'click' as the section swung outwards a few inches. She pulled and the whole four foot section swung silently open on well-oiled hinges. Light spilling over her shoulder showed a dark space in front of her.

On the left of wall of the hidden space was a light switch. Ellen flipped it on and leaned in. The space was four feet deep and ran the length of the study behind the bookshelves. Glancing over her shoulder Ellen entered the hidden room and pulled the bookshelf closed after her. The wall opposite the back of the bookshelves was the empty. The back side of the shelves was bare except for a tiny bit of light halfway down. At the opposite end of the space from where she stood was a table with several items on it.

There were two paintings leaning against the long wall. Ellen took a closer look at one. It was an amazingly bright landscape colored with brilliant swirls of paint. In the lower corner was a signature that read *Cezanne*. The other one was signed *Matisse*. Ellen frowned. She didn't know enough about art to decide if these were originals or fakes but they looked good. If they were real; why hide them in a closet? If they were fakes; why have them at all? Were they stolen? Payoff for blackmail? Tabling those thoughts, she turned toward the table.

Reaching out she turned on a goose neck lamp to illuminate the table at the far end of the space. There was a map taped to the wall above the table. The map was of greater L.A. with pins stuck in several locations. On the table was a loaded revolver that she looked at carefully but did not touch. There was a stack of papers and files. She sorted through them being careful with fingerprints. All of them contained information on various local businesses and local unions. All circumstantial evidence but not what she was looking for. There was also a telephone. The number on the card at its base was the one Travis had given her: the hidden phone.

Moving a chair aside Ellen looked under the table. There was a foot locker sized metal chest closed with a hasp and padlock. This was more like it. Pulling up her long blue gown she removed a piece of metal sewn into the hem of it. Using the lock pick she made quick work of the padlock. It clicked open in less than two minutes. Inside was another revolver several more files, a ledger and a boat load of cash. Ellen smiled: bingo!

She picked up the ledger and opened it up on the desk. Tucked inside the cover was a handwritten list of names, addresses and phone numbers. The top name on the list was *Joseph Travis*. Ellen had no doubt that this was a list of the hoods working for Monteaux. The ledger itself was filled with pages of names, dates and figures. Protection money paid to Monteaux without doubt. Here was all the evidence she needed.

It occurred to Ellen that it was now high time for her to be elsewhere. She re-locked the box and turned off the light but before she opened the hidden door she put her eye to the tiny patch of light in the back of the shelves. Someone had cut a hole through to allow view of the outer room. It was empty. She quickly left the room and re-entered the study closing the hidden door behind her. Brushing her gown to make sure it had picked up no dirt she palmed the lock pick and was turning toward the door when she heard laughter on the other side of it.

Quickly she scooted to the drinks table and picked up a bottle and glass. She poured a drink just as the door opened and Monteaux entered with an attractive young girl on his arm. He stared in surprise at Ellen, "Ellen. I'm uh…" She smiled and glided up to him, "I thought we might have that drink we talked about. But, I see you're busy." She then squeezed past him whispering in his ear as she did, "Perhaps another time." Out in the hallway she made her way upstairs sipping her drink and congratulating herself on her good timing.

Upstairs it took a few minutes to locate Joanne. She was sitting very close to a well-known movie producer and talking very earnestly to him. Ellen interrupted and apologized. She pleaded a sudden migraine and need to leave. Joanne assured her friend that she would have no trouble getting a ride home. Ellen then left quietly. She had a lot to think about on the trip home.

Long after midnight the next night, a white clad figure pulled her black cloak tighter around her and moved through the shadows near Monteaux's house. The Domino Lady eventually arrived at the French doors leading to Monteaux's darkened study. The doors were locked but three minutes work with her picks opened the lock so she could slip inside. The dim moonlight streaming through the doors gave her enough light to open the bookcase and enter Monteaux's lair.

Using a small flashlight she quickly opened the chest and removed several thick bundles of cash. She also opened the ledger and removed the list of Monteaux's hoods. That she replaced in the chest. She then placed one of her black calling cards on top of the list before quickly relocking it.

Carrying the ledger she quickly left the hidden room and the study. She relocked the French doors and a few minutes later was motoring quietly away in her roadster. As she drove home she thought about the final phase of her plan.

The next day was Monday. Ellen made her preparations and after a quick stop at a post office branch she was in front of Roberts' office by noon. She followed him when he went to lunch and then back to his office. She left him there and drove quickly to his apartment. She parked down the street and made her way to his building. The lobby was open and she climbed unnoticed to the second floor. It too was empty and she made quick work of the lock on his door.

Inside she opened her overly large purse and pulled out several bundles of cash that she had liberated from Monteaux's stash. She smiled at the thought of Monteaux. A couple of hours before, she had made an anonymous call to the police. Requesting to speak to the detective in charge of the Griffith Park kidnapping she proceeded to give him all the information she had on Monteaux and his operations. She told him about the secret room in his house, the cash, the records and the paintings that he had hidden there. She also told him that more evidence had been mailed to police headquarters and should be there soon. When the detective had demanded to know who she was and how she knew all this she had just laughed and hung up on him.

Certain now that Monteaux would have police crawling all over his life; she turned her attention to Roberts. She broke open the bundles of money taken from Monteaux and spread nearly thirty thousand dollars around on his coffee table. She looked at her handiwork appraisingly. She quickly made up several stacks of identical domination bills as if someone was counting it. Satisfied she made an anonymous call to the local office of the IRS. When the phone was answered Ellen spoke, "The police have just caught Douglas Roberts with a huge amount of cash hidden at his apartment. If I were you I'd go see what's going on." As the agent on the other end of the telephone sputtered in surprise, she hung up with a smile.

Ellen then had the operator connect her with the police. When a voice came on the line she yelled in a slightly hysterical voice, "You've got to get over here quick I think he's killing her! She's screaming something terrible!"

The policeman on other end of the phone spoke loudly, "Slow down ma'am! What's the address there?"

Ellen gave the policeman the address and Roberts' apartment number. She then screamed once and yelled, "Oh my god! Did you hear that?" She quickly hung up. Ellen figured she had about five minutes but she still moved quickly. She wiped the door knobs and anything else she had touched. She left the apartment with the front door ajar and carefully placed a twenty dollar bill in the half open doorway.

Out on the street she walked casually to her roadster and sat inside. She didn't have to wait long. Very soon a squad car pulled up outside Roberts' apartment and two uniformed officers hurried inside. A few minutes later another car pulled up and a man in a suit got out. He was met by one of the uniforms and escorted inside. Several minutes passed and Ellen looked at her watch. Roberts should be showing up anytime after pretending to do some "honest" work at his office. Sure enough fifteen minutes later Roberts parked just behind the two police cars and got out. He stopped and peered thoughtfully at the cars for a moment before turning and walking away. He was quickly stopped by an officer who came out of the apartment building. He was then escorted inside.

Ellen smiled. It looked like Monteaux's stolen money was going to do some good after all. She was now sure that both Monteaux and Roberts would get the justice they deserved. As she started her car another sedan pulled up behind Roberts' car and two men got out and entered the building. Ellen nodded as she pulled away; those two had the look of government men if she had ever seen any.

Two days later, Ellen sipped her champagne and set the empty glass on the floor next to the bathtub. She then continued reading the story on page one of that morning's *Times*. It told of the arrest of George Monteaux on a multitude of charges. She nodded and thought about the remainder of the money she had taken from Monteaux's chest. There were some needy charities that would put it to good use. Right now her only problem was that her glass was empty and the champagne bottle was in the kitchen. Aaarrggh!

The End

CALIFORNIA GIRLS
Part 2

So having completed *Over a Barrel* I sat down to come up with a companion story for the new Domino Lady anthology. I knew I wanted to move the setting back to Southern California and I also wanted more of that glamorous feeling that makes Domino Lady so much fun. I also wanted lots of easily identifiable California locations. Since I didn't have a lot of space for a complicated plot I also decided that a good action opening sequence would set the pace for a quick adventure.

Looking for inspiration, I dug through my movies set in the 1930s and voila' I came across *The Rocketeer,* a movie it had been far too long since I had watched. So I sat down to an enjoyable two hours of rollicking 1930's adventure. The climax of that wonderful film takes place at one of the most easily identifiable Los Angeles locations: Griffith Park Observatory. That was just what I was looking for, especially since my story would fall during the years when it was being constructed. Perfect.

I had already determined that this second story would have a good chunk of action it. So, a slam bam action sequence in Griffith Park followed by a high speed run through Hollywood seemed a perfect opening. The rest was half Domino Lady seduction and half set up of the bad guys. What can I say? *Open Grave* then practically wrote itself. I wrote the first half in a day and a half and it was a ton of fun. It was a bit dark but it gave me a chance to write the scene for which the story is named. For me the Domino Lady is at her best when she is tricking information out of her foes. Her wits are a far more potent weapon than her pistol or even her trusty syringe. In the end I went back and lightened the scene slightly but still retained the mood I was looking for.

The second half of the story was classic Domino Lady. She is busy either seducing bad guys or sneaking around where she's not supposed to be. In the end *Open Grave* came out just as I planned; a short, fun adventure with a good bit of action seasoned with the usual Domino Lady antics. As with *Over a Barrel* I managed to work in some classic California settings. In addition to Griffith Park all the streets are just where they are supposed to be and I also found a place for the famous *Formosa* restaurant, a Los Angeles landmark since it was built in 1929. You might remember it from a scene in *LA Confidential,* one of the best detective noir films about Los Angeles ever made, in my humble opinion.

123

Some writing is hard, some is easy. Domino Lady writing comes easy for me. I have written enough Domino Lady stories to feel very comfortable with her. I hope it shows in these latest stories. I have to thank Ron Fortier for helping me with my story dilemma. He made it possible for me to once again make an appearance in the latest Domino Lady adventure. I would have hated to miss it. My only problem now is figuring out what I'm going to do for volume 4???

Thanks for reading both *Over a Barrel* and *Open Grave.* I hope you enjoyed reading them as much as I enjoyed writing them and I hope to be back for the next volume.

GENE MOYERS - studied European and Medieval history at the University of Oregon. He is also a U.S. Army veteran. He worked in the high tech industry for some time and ran a store front and internet hobby shop for several years.

An avid military gamer and role player, his favorite game was *Daredevils* a pulp based roleplaying game set in the 1930s. His love affair with the 1930s and pulps in particular stem from his first time reading a *Shadow* novel as a boy. Although interested in writing since a teen he did not turn to serious writing until 2000.

He is the co-author of *GURPS Crusades* published by Steve Jackson Games.He has now written several stories for Airship 27 including stories published in *Ravenwood vol. 2, The Purple Scar vol. 1, The Domino Lady vol. 1, Black Bat vol. 3, The Phantom Detective vol. 1* and *The Legends of New Pulp Fiction.* He has also written soon to be published stories for both Moonstone Books and Pro Se Press.

When not working on various new pulp projects he is busy writing horror adventures for his colonial swashbuckler. Gene currently lives in Beaverton, Oregon with his wife and two lazy dogs.

THE DOMINO LADY TAKES THE CASE

by Samantha Lienhard

Over the past few months, Ellen Patrick had visited the Ambrose home on many occasions, but never under such somber circumstances. She sipped the tea she'd been offered and studied the woman across from her.

Nancy Ambrose wore all black. Her fingers trembled around her teacup. "Thank you for coming, Ellen. I know I'm not good company right now."

"Don't even think you need to apologize." Ellen reached out with one delicate, pink-nailed hand and patted the other woman's arm. "I'll do anything I can to help."

Her companion managed a weak smile, but shook her head. "It was so sudden. One minute, Daniel and I were making plans, and then the next…" She trailed off with a choked sob.

Sudden indeed, and all the more suspicious because of it. Daniel Ambrose had a promising career and a bright future. When his body was discovered in an isolated alley, riddled with bullets, it came as a shock to everyone who knew him. He was a mild-mannered, discreet man, not the sort to get himself mixed up in danger.

Unless, of course, that danger came from a source most people wouldn't expect.

"Do the police have any clues?" Ellen asked, keeping her tone as calm as if she merely wished to help her acquaintance find closure.

"They believe he got mixed up with the mob. They said they're close to finding out who did it."

An all-too convenient explanation. While it might seem logical to the public, to Ellen it reeked of a cover-up. Daniel had been investigating crimes in his free time—crimes related to the corrupt political machine that had stolen many innocent lives before his. Answers lay there, she was sure of it.

"They don't think it had anything to do with his investigations?" she asked.

Nancy shook her head. "I know he said he was digging up corruption, but the police haven't found a connection. They looked through all of his

125

notes already and found no credible leads."

"His notes?"

If the other woman noticed the gleam of interest in Ellen's brown eyes, she didn't comment on it. But of course, how could she ever suspect that the young debutante in front of her had an interest in Daniel's work, or indeed, that such matters were what lead her to first contact the Ambroses? With her lovely golden curls and petite frame, Ellen looked as harmless as any of the countless other society women in Southland.

"Daniel was always taking notes," Nancy said with a sad laugh. "Always staying up in that office of his, looking through records, searching for patterns… And for what? Nothing."

Ellen affected a wide-eyed look of alarm, only partly feigned. "Surely the police can't have searched all of his notes already." Less than twenty-four hours had passed since the murder, not nearly enough time for a thorough inspection of his research.

"They said they'll return if they find any new evidence."

Return? Then the notes remained in the house. Ellen hesitated. The part of her that longed for justice and vengeance burned with the need to read those notes. Yet there was no good reason for Ellen Patrick to demand access to Daniel's office. At best, it would alarm her grieving acquaintance. At worst, she would mention it to the police when they next visited.

Ellen's experiences with the police had left her with little faith in them, aside from a trusted few.

"I'm sure they'll bring the killer to justice," she said instead. "Is there anything I can do for you, dear?"

Nancy shook her head. "I don't know, I don't know. I can't think straight. Nothing seems right anymore."

"I'll help out as much as I can."

"There are so many things going on—oh, and the party! We were supposed to have a party." She threw her hands in the air. "Doesn't it seem absurd, to discuss a party at a time like this? Yet it was to be such a grand occasion, with such high-profile guests…" Tears filled her eyes. "And Daniel was looking forward to it, too. I've never seen him so eager to entertain. He kept emphasizing how important it was. He even sent out the invitations himself. It meant so much to him, I feel like he'd want me to go ahead with it, but…"

Curious. Daniel Ambrose never spent much time in high society, despite his social status. If he was fixated on this particular event, perhaps it was worth looking into.

"It's a wonderful way to honor his memory," Ellen said. "Don't worry. We'll all be there to support you."

"Thank you."

For the rest of the day, she helped Nancy get things back into order in her husband's absence and did her best to be a supportive friend and comforting listener. Not once did she let her gaze stray toward the office. She needed that information, but not as Ellen Patrick.

This was a job for the Domino Lady.

When evening fell, Ellen once again approached the house where the late Daniel Ambrose kept his notes, but this time in secrecy. She wore a backless white frock that clung to her shapely figure, with a black cape draped across her shoulders and gloves concealing her hands. As for her face, the upper half was obscured by a black silk domino mask.

For though it would have given her acquaintance quite a shock to know the truth, Ellen Patrick was none other than the notorious Domino Lady!

The lovely vigilante sometimes accepted jobs for the sake of friendship, other times to satisfy her lust for adventure, but most often to root out corruption. When those goals overlapped, as they did in this case, so much the better.

She paused to survey the house. The lights were out. Poor Nancy was no doubt struggling to fall asleep in her empty bedroom, stricken by the loss of her husband. Yet while grief might distract her, fear born from her husband's fate might also make her alert for any small sound. Ellen would have to move carefully.

Not that the Domino Lady was ever one to shy away from a challenge. If anything, it added to the thrill.

A compact folding jimmy retrieved from her wrist bag made short work of the lock, and she slipped silently inside. Silence hung over the house. No sign of anyone who might disturb her. She carefully made her way to the office.

It was unlocked. She scanned the room for any sign of a trap and then shut herself inside. Clear moonlight from the window provided enough light to see by.

The last time she stood in this office was when she met Daniel for the first time. She'd expressed interest in his theories about political corruption in the city, and he went on for quite some time before laughing it off as something she surely wouldn't be interested in. She'd joined his laughter, all while thinking that here was an ally she could count on in her secret struggle, a true kindred spirit.

And so he'd been silenced, just as a bullet silenced her father so many years earlier. Ellen clenched her fists. The memory still fueled the deep fury that led her to become the Domino Lady.

Her life had been well on track for other things. Once, the demure image most people had of Ellen Patrick was no myth. After graduating from Berkeley, she spent some time in the Far East, and no doubt would have been married and settled in the following years if her return home hadn't been spurred by the tragic news.

After her father's death, she dedicated her life to destroying everyone responsible and dismantling the corrupt political machine one piece at a time. Wishing things turned out differently accomplished nothing, not for her father and not for poor Daniel. Only action would solve this. Daniel had been a strong potential ally. His murderer would pay.

She walked to the large desk at the center of the room and turned her attention to the papers on top.

Daniel Ambrose was diligent in his work, to say the least. He had records on nearly everything related to politics from the local level to the state. It appeared he obtained all of his information legitimately—leading to transcripts of conversations, public records, and files dating back years from all across California and even from other states as well. To search through it all for patterns and contradictions, he must have spent hours combing over every document. No wonder the police were reluctant to review his work.

Ellen's brief flash of sympathy vanished. If the police chose to ignore potential evidence just because it was tedious, she had no respect for them.

Besides, there had to be something more clear-cut. Daniel's scribbles in the margins couldn't be all he had. She crouched and opened the first desk drawer. Similar papers and documents to those on top… In the second drawer, papers related to personal matters… And in the third, a series of four thick leather-bound journals.

She picked up the first one.

Yes, this was what she needed, Daniel's own notes and thoughts on his investigation! With any luck, she would find a clue to point her toward the murderer. Eagerly, she began to read.

Distant sirens sent a jolt through her. She crept to the office window and peered out. Flashing lights approached the house.

It was too much to hope they weren't coming there. Nancy must have heard something. Ellen glanced at the journal in her hand. It was too early to make a blatant move, when she had yet to know who her enemy was. The disappearance of the journals might draw too much attention—and possibly alert the mysterious killer that the Domino Lady was on his trail.

She needed to act quickly.

As the sirens grew louder, Ellen paged through the first journal. Clearly Daniel's early notes, where a pattern had yet to show itself. She moved onto the next. Certain names began to appear more frequently. The next! Time was running out, but she couldn't leave until she had an idea of what Daniel suspected.

The final journal was the most fruitful, as his theories and connections took shape. He saw corruption everywhere; that much was clear, but which of his targets could have feared his investigation enough to silence him?

Outside, the sirens stopped. There was a sharp knocking, followed by Nancy's voice. "Yes, officer, I know I heard something. I don't know what it sounded like—but someone was down here, I'm sure of it!"

Ellen drew a sharp breath. She hastened through the remaining pages.

"Take a look outside. We'll check the downstairs."

There, a name that repeated itself again and again. *Gerald Wilson.* Whoever he was, he had significantly attracted Daniel's attention before his death. Enough to lead to murder?

"Is there anything a burglar would have been after?"

"I don't know, but"—Nancy sounded breathless, nearly hysterical—"my husband was just murdered, after all. Could it be related to that? He still has those papers in his office. When you were here before, you said you didn't think they were connected, but—"

Time was up.

Ellen returned the journals to the drawer and slid it silently shut. Then she crept to the window. Outside, two police officers searched the grounds. Her heart skipped a beat. They were close. They'd notice for sure if she opened the window.

She moved toward the door instead and crouched with her ear pressed against the wood. Footsteps approached, far too fast.

Her gaze darted from side to side, but there were no hiding places she might easily use. Desperate, she flattened herself against the wall alongside the door, and held her breath. At least the moonlight had served her well; there was no lamp on to arouse their suspicions.

"It's unlocked," someone said just outside the door. "Did you leave it that way?"

Nancy sounded like she was on the brink of hysteria. "Yes, I think so. No one told me to lock it! You said it wasn't important!"

Guilt made Ellen bow her head. She disliked causing further distress to the widow, even if her intentions were ultimately to help her. While she befriended the Ambroses to learn more about Daniel's work, she'd grown fond of his wife during their time together. She would have to pay Nancy a visit soon again, to see if there was anything she could do.

The door flew open, nearly crushing the Domino Lady. Fortunately, her petite frame let her fit neatly in the gap left between door and wall. Breath held, she only prayed they didn't close the door again and see her.

One police officer stepped into the office. He looked from side to side and then walked around the desk. "No sign of any intruders." He examined the window. "Locked. No one went out this way."

Body trembling, lungs burning from lack of breath, Ellen remained as still as possible.

After one last look around, the officer left. The door swung shut, and Ellen was alone again. She let out a gasping breath and leaned against the wall to steady herself; chest heaving beneath her silk gown.

Close call or not, it had been worth it. She had a name. Gerald Wilson, a mysterious man who had attracted Daniel's attention shortly before his murder. And thanks to Nancy, she knew of one other thing that had gotten the murdered man's interest around the same time.

Perhaps Gerald Wilson would be in attendance at the party.

"Thank you for coming." Nancy looked better than she had a week earlier, although she still wore black and her face was wan. "You've been such a help to me."

Ellen waved off her thanks. "I promised I would be here, didn't I?"

In a pale blue gown, a pastel shade that complemented her pink-painted fingernails, and with her golden curls left to hang loose around her face, Ellen looked a far cry from the vigilante who crept through these same halls not a week past. Wrist bag in hand, she followed Nancy into the grand parlor where the party was to take place.

"There are so many people here," she said, her gaze on the guests who had already arrived. Some were familiar from her many contacts in high society, but others were strangers, hopefully the suspects she and Daniel both sought.

"I'll introduce you."

Nancy approached each of her guests to ask about their experiences, and Ellen stayed by her side. Many knew her already, or at least knew *of* her—newspapers often covered stories about the beautiful young debutante. To the rest, she let herself be introduced and listened for the name she wanted to hear.

A few names appeared in Daniel's journal, names to keep in mind for the future, because even if they didn't play a role in his death, they might be involved in something else.

Then, at last—

"Ellen, I'd like you to meet Gerald Wilson and his son, Walter."

She extended her hand and greeted them with a polite smile, the image of a young woman eager to make further connections in the upper echelons of society. At the same time, her eyes narrowed with curiosity. Gerald Wilson was a large man, with streaks of white at his temples and a face set in the typical politician's mask, a friendly smile to mask his true intentions.

The younger man was different. Nearly as tall as his father, Walter Wilson had jet-black hair and a lean, muscular frame. He looked bored as they approached, but when introduced to Ellen, his face became open, almost naïve in how little effort he put forth to hide his interest.

His gaze darted over Ellen in her attractive, clinging gown. "I am quite pleased to meet you, Miss Patrick."

She chuckled and offered him a coy smile of her own as she took his hand. "The pleasure is all mine, Mr. Wilson."

Then they moved on to the next guests, but Ellen's mind raced toward a plan. The younger Wilson's attraction to her could be used to her advantage—and unless he was as corrupt as his father, it would be enjoyable work, as well. He might be the key piece she needed to learn about Gerald's history and potential for murder.

After they finished their circuit of the parlor, Nancy returned to the door to greet the latest guests. "The young men seem quite smitten with you, Ellen."

A perfect lead-in. Ellen smiled and fanned herself. "Particularly Walter... what did you say his last name was again?"

"Wilson, Walter Wilson." Nancy laughed. "Leave it to you to catch his eye after only just meeting him. I don't know how you do it."

"Is his family important? I can't say I've heard their name before."

That was the strangest part of all. After her visit to Daniel's office as the Domino Lady, Ellen had spent the past week researching the name she uncovered—and the result was almost nothing. Gerald Wilson didn't seem to be a public figure, yet not only had he attracted Daniel's attention, but Nancy spoke of him as though he was important.

"They're quite wealthy," Nancy said. She greeted another guest and then turned back to Ellen, her voice a hushed whisper. "I've heard Gerald Wilson is a political boss, but I don't know if it's true or not. He seems to be a very private man."

"Interesting. And Walter?"

"He's a businessman. From what I understand, his father started the company, but turned it over to him in order to pursue his own interests."

"How fascinating. Perhaps he'll tell me more about it."

So Gerald Wilson was some sort of secret political boss, pulling strings from the shadows while leaving few records that tied directly back to him. Ah, what she would have given to see Daniel's journal again, but for the moment that was too dangerous a course to take. All that paperwork must have paid off in the end and provided a trail leading to Daniel's elusive quarry.

Ellen said her farewells to Nancy and made her way back through the parlor in pursuit of her lead. After all, while she could enjoy the pleasures of a social event as much as anyone, this particular gathering served a far more important purpose.

Guests greeted her as she passed. Mindful of her public appearance, she played her role well. They spoke of casual matters and exchanged quiet lamentations about the somber circumstances surrounding the party, and she moved on from group to group until she found herself face-to-face with her potential lead.

"You look like you're in need of company," Walter said.

With a smile, Ellen turned to face him. "I'm afraid I'm a bit out of place at events like this. There's hardly a soul here I know."

"Are you enjoying yourself?"

"Oh yes."

"Then we should trade places." With a hearty chuckle, Walter waved his hand at the crowd. "I know almost all of these people from past occasions, yet I wish I could stay at home."

"You don't enjoy parties?"

"Not these parties. Dull conversation, bland niceties… of course, it's not at every party that I meet you."

"Is that why you came?" she asked, with a shy smile and flirtatious air that masked the way her thoughts blurred into action at the curious announcement that the political boss's son disliked the grand social events to which they were invited. "You knew you would meet me here?"

"That was merely a wonderful coincidence, or perhaps destiny." He sighed and shook his head. "No, I came because it's an obligation."

"For your company?"

"Mainly for Father. He thinks it's important that I attend these things."

"Is your father a businessman too?" she asked with a wide-eyed look of curiosity.

"Father helps people. He's a consultant."

"A consultant?" That was either a curious way to disguise his work as a political boss, or he'd actually told his own son a false story about his job. "You mean he advises other companies?"

"Yes, something like that. I don't want to bore you with the details, though." Walter cleared his throat. "May I get you a drink?"

"Thank you." Ellen accepted the drink when he returned with it with a shy smile. "And don't worry about boring me. I'm sure anything you have to say will be interesting.

Twenty minutes later, Ellen knew about all the ins and outs of Walter's business. A few casual questions had earned her the names of various politicians and their ilk who "consulted" his father, though he seemed entirely disinterested in the topic. He was apparently both in the dark about his father's ties to politics and in desperate need of someone to talk to.

"…and events like this aren't strictly necessary, if you ask me, but Father says it's important that I make appearances. So I do it, if only to make him happy."

"I'm pleased you did this time," Ellen said.

"For once, so am I." Walter smiled at her, then gave himself a shake. "I'm sorry, have I been going on all this time? I must have bored you."

"Not at all."

"It's all right. You don't need to lie out of respect for me. I've been told many times that I'm a very dull person."

Ellen lifted her eyebrows. Walter was turning out to be most unusual. The more she listened to him, the more she doubted he had anything to do with his father's corruption. Despite his success in business, he seemed innocent in many ways. She initially assumed he would be nothing more than a lead to get her more information on Gerald, but she couldn't deny her personal curiosity in someone who seemed so out of place at this event.

And he was hardly unattractive. Under other circumstances, she wouldn't mind his company, and if the current situation made it a bit manipulative, well, no harm should come to him if he was innocent. Sympathy for the son would not stand in the way of taking down the father, especially if Gerald was the murderer she sought.

That was key. All she had so far was tangential evidence, not enough for even her to conclude definitively that he killed Daniel.

"I don't think you're dull at all," she said to Walter with a shy smile. "I hope I'll get to see you again."

"I certainly hope so as well."

"Perhaps next time we'll meet at a venue more to your liking."

That evening, Ellen outlined everything she knew about Gerald Wilson and his potential connection to Daniel Ambrose, safe from prying eyes in the security of her own home.

It was indeed a luxurious place, and at first glance, one might be puzzled about how a young woman on her own afforded such a lifestyle. But while work as a secret vigilante did not always come with the thanks it deserved, it did have its benefits. Most of the money Ellen claimed from her targets went to charity and other good causes, but she kept a small fraction for herself to ensure she lived comfortably and to fund her future operations.

Yes, it was a good cycle, and it would never end—at least not until she crushed the corrupt system that led to her father's death!

One piece at a time, she took them down, but there would always be more corruption, more blackmail, more villains who couldn't be touched by the law. And then there were the police, all too willing to turn a blind eye in certain situations. Ellen sometimes handled jobs merely to make fools out of the men who never sought justice for her father.

Perhaps being the Domino Lady was a job for life, but it was hers by choice and she would never give up.

As Ellen looked over the information she gathered, the pieces began to take shape. Gerald was even more central to things than she initially thought.

And he was hardly unattractive.

He not only aided corrupt politicians, but he enabled or even encouraged their corruption! This became apparent when she examined the behavior of certain politicians before and after their "consultations" with the elder Wilson. No wonder Daniel's notes contained such extensive descriptions.

To keep his own power intact from the shadows, Gerald put men in positions of power through means that kept them indebted to him… loyalty that was one part gratitude and two parts fear; he gave them their positions and obtained the means to blackmail them at the same time.

There were many people the Domino Lady might need to pay a visit to in the future, and once again Ellen wished she had Daniel's journals. But again, one piece at a time. They could wait until the murderer was found and detained.

Had Daniel's investigation led him too close to the truth about Gerald? If so, had he done the deed personally, or did he merely give the order?

Walter might be the path to the answers she needed.

"You've been spending a lot of time with Walter, haven't you?" Nancy asked.

"Yes." Ellen smiled. "I've grown fond of him."

In the two weeks since the party, Walter had called on her several times and showered her with expensive gifts as tokens of his affection. They went for walks together, enjoyed a boat ride, and even attended another one of the parties he dreaded, where she kept an eye on the people meeting with Gerald and learned a few more details from Walter.

Every time, she gained another shred of information about his father. Gerald had been in contact with Daniel before his death. On the night Daniel died, Gerald went to a private retreat along the coast where he liked to spend time alone—making his whereabouts unverifiable.

The more Ellen learned, the more sure she became convinced Gerald Wilson was the murderer. But how to catch him? Nothing she'd learned would work for a police force already determined to steer the investigation away from such an influential figure.

"I'm glad something good came out of the party," Nancy said. "Daniel would be pleased."

Indeed, no doubt he'd be delighted to see someone picking up where he left off and seeking justice for him. "How are you doing?" Ellen asked. "Are the police making any progress?"

Nancy sighed. "They think they've found the culprit."

Ellen kept her voice calm, despite her flash of panic. "They have?"

"Some two-bit gangster known for having a hot temper, from the way they've described the situation. It's not certain yet, but they said it shouldn't take too much longer. I can't imagine what Daniel was thinking to get mixed up with someone like that…"

Such a criminal sounded like the perfect scapegoat. Ellen had no love for organized crime, but less love for false convictions. Letting the police frame this man for the murder would let the true killer go free.

The Domino Lady was running out of time.

"It was good of you to come on such short notice."

Ellen let a smile be her answer as Walter greeted her from the mansion's antechamber. The servant who had answered the door stepped aside to let her pass. Despite the many evenings she and Walter spent together already, this was her first visit to his home. The Wilson mansion was a large structure, impressive from the outside with elaborate architecture and an expansive lawn, and just as impressive on the inside from her initial look. The antechamber they walked through was as dazzling as the parlors in other houses.

"Follow me," Walter said.

He led her into a large entrance hall, with doors off the sides and a large staircase in the center that went up to the second and third floors. Their shoes clicked against the marble floor. She couldn't help but notice the number of potted plants that adorned the entrance hall. Someone in the mansion clearly liked them quite a bit.

"Father's office is on the second floor."

Ellen followed him up the stairs. Gerald's sudden request to meet her again had taken her by surprise. For all his influence, even he couldn't know she was the Domino Lady; she held that secret so tightly that almost no one knew the truth. Yet she had been asking many questions about him, and while her inquiries were subtle enough to avoid rousing Walter's suspicions, his father's political savvy might have helped him put the pieces together.

Such a situation might easily have caused trepidation, but for the young adventuress, it instead filled her with a thrill of excitement. What awaited her in Gerald's office—another clue to bring her plans together or a hammer prepared to shatter them apart? She would soon find out.

She counted the doors as they walked along the blue carpeting at the top of the stairs. Knowing the location of Gerald's office could prove vital.

Walter stopped in front of a door made from polished ebony oak. He knocked once, then opened it and stepped aside. Ellen glanced at him, and after he waved his hand for her to go ahead, she strode into the office. He closed the door behind her.

Gerald stood looking out the large open window, but he turned when she entered. He nodded. "Please take a seat, Miss Patrick." After one last glance outside, he sat in the large leather chair behind his desk.

Another chair sat facing him, presumably for any guests. Ellen sat down. She held her wrist bag in her lap, clasped primly between her hands. Her pink-painted fingernails glistened in the light, and to anyone who looked, she would appear to be a harmless young woman unused to dealing with the world of politics and corruption—an impression she certainly hoped to convey to Gerald.

His office was the sort of elaborate room one would expect from someone of his means. Everything had a veneer of quality that hinted at its high worth without being blatant about it, and the walls were accented with gold. Yet two things took her by surprise. First, more leafy plants sat in the corners and others hung from the ceiling, creating a veritable jungle behind his desk. All the plants downstairs were his choice, then.

Second, amid the opulence of his office, portraits and paintings stood out in sharp contrast, because they were all of his family. Portraits of Walter as a child and a young man, even more of a pale young woman who must be Walter's mother, and several that showed the three of them together.

How could a man be engaged in such corruption and yet show such love for his family?

Gerald studied her, his expression unreadable. "I'm afraid I don't know much about you, Miss Patrick, although I've heard your name before."

"We met at Nancy Ambrose's party."

"Yes, I know that, but it was such a brief meeting and I was introduced to so many people."

"I went to support Nancy." Ellen lowered her head, but surreptitiously watched Gerald for his reaction. "After Daniel passed away, I wanted to be there for her."

He flinched. "Yes, what happened to him truly was unfortunate."

"Did you know him well?"

"Not well, no. We merely had some business exchanges." Gerald cleared his throat. "But I did not call you here to discuss such sad topics."

Interesting. He clearly didn't want to talk about Daniel. Tempted though she was to press him further, Ellen kept her mouth shut. Arousing Gerald's suspicions would prove disastrous.

"Even in the darkest of times," he said, "there is some light. You met Walter at that party, and now you're the only girl he talks about. He's quite taken with you, Miss Patrick."

She lifted her head. In the end, was the true purpose of this meeting merely a father concerned about his son's choice of companions? Ah, if he only knew the truth about her motives. The thought made her smile.

"You appear to be a fine young woman," Gerald said. "From what I understand, you're on your own. Is that true?"

"My father died several years ago. He was all I had."

"I see." The older man bowed his head for a moment. "I lost my wife many years ago, as well." He sighed. "To someone in your position, a match such as Walter must look quite appealing."

"Goodness, that's not what this is." Ellen lifted her hand in protest as indignation welled up within her. The nerve of him to think she'd be interested in his son for his money. "My father left me well-off, and I have done fine for myself. Please, Mr. Wilson, do not assume the worst of me."

Then again, she could hardly blame him. Someone mired in greed, for whom money and power determined every course of action, must certainly ascribe the same motivations to the people around him.

He regarded her for a moment and then nodded. "Forgive me, Miss Patrick. He's my only son. I'm quite protective of him."

"I understand."

"Still, he might seem like an ideal match for any—"

A sudden crashing sound cut him off. Ellen jumped and looked around for the source of the ruckus, only to realize it came from the open window.

Gerald sighed and rose from behind his desk. "As much as I enjoy the fresh air, I should remember to keep the window shut when I have guests." He closed the window, which silenced the noise, and then turned to her with an apologetic smile. "You must forgive the interruption. This is a fine house, but it has a few peculiarities."

"Noise from the grounds carries up here?"

"Worse, from the parlor." He shook his head. "My office is unfortunately positioned above one of our parlors, and when both windows are open at once, the sound carries."

"How dreadful."

"Ah, but it has its benefits." He winked.

Ellen tilted her head. "It does?"

"The parlor below my office is ideal. It's grand and luxurious, the perfect place for guests to stop and talk. So you see, with the windows open, I can often overhear conversations not meant for my ears."

What a horrible trick. Yet at the same time, it might prove useful. "Does that mean that whoever's down there might have been listening in on our conversation, too?" she asked, eyes wide.

"Yes, and I apologize. Although it's not as though we discussed anything confidential." He chuckled. "Your involvement with Walter is far from a secret."

She blushed and looked away as if in embarrassment. Inwardly, her heart sang with triumph. This unusual construction of the Wilson mansion might be exactly what she needed to bring Gerald to justice.

"I do apologize if I caused you any offense with my earlier comment," he said.

"It's fine."

"But I should warn you that the time may come when a different match becomes necessary, and I don't want to see a fine young woman like you get hurt because of it, particularly since my son lacks certain... social graces."

She frowned. "Are you implying that he might cast me aside in favor of someone else?"

"It's a possibility you need to be prepared for."

"Wouldn't that be his decision, not yours?"

"Yes. He would be the one to decide."

Ellen bristled, irritated on Walter's behalf as well as her own. "I don't think you know the sort of man he is."

"Perhaps that's true," Gerald said with a sigh. "Sometimes, I don't understand him at all."

"Whatever happens, I'm prepared to deal with it."

"I see." He held out his hand. "I am pleased we had this chance to talk. If you and Walter continue to spend time together, I look forward to seeing you here again."

She accepted his handshake. "I'm certain we'll see each other more often."

"You said your father is gone? Then think of me as your father. You can come to me whenever you need help or advice, no matter what the situation is."

"Thank you."

Ellen stood and walked to the door. On one hand, this meeting resulted in no new information about Gerald. On the other hand, he appeared to have no suspicions as to her true intentions. If anything, he seemed concerned for her well-being.

His offer of advice puzzled her. He didn't seem like that sort of man. Was there something else he wanted? Just one more piece to the puzzle.

Walter greeted her the moment she left the office. "Is everything all right?"

"Yes," she said with a smile. "Your father just wanted to get to know me better."

Despite his shady dealings and cynical outlook, Gerald showed genuine concern when it came to his son's welfare. Even the corrupt weren't pure evil.

"Thank God." Walter let out a sigh of relief. "I worried when he called you in there that he might—well, that he might have a reason to disapprove."

She tilted her head. "Like what?"

"Oh, nothing in particular. As long as he didn't say anything offensive to you or try to drive you away, then everything is fine. Father can be overprotective."

"He did seem concerned that you might break my heart."

Walter met her gaze. "That, I will never do." He looked into her eyes a moment longer, until her cheeks heated, and then he cleared his throat. "Enough of that. Please, let me show you around before you leave."

"Thank you. I'd like that."

Although she'd hoped to see more of the second floor's layout, he led her down the stairs to the first floor and led her from room to room. The mansion was as large as she imagined from its exterior. He showed her a dining area, a ballroom, and chamber after chamber until she could scarcely believe they hadn't seen the whole thing, yet she could tell it was only a small fraction of the whole. Inwardly she focused on memorizing the mansion's layout.

"Do you like music?" he asked; as they walked down a hallway that branched off from the entrance hall.

"I love it."

"Then you'll enjoy this." He opened a door and led her inside.

Ellen couldn't withhold a gasp. It was a beautiful music room, with a grand piano set up in the center, a harpsichord against the wall, and more.

Walter walked to the piano and sat at it.

She sat in the armchair across from the piano. "I didn't know you played."

"I even compose some of my own music."

"That's wonderful."

He beamed and began to play. For the next hour, Ellen simply sat and listened. The lovely melodies carried her far from the grim reality of her situation. When he finished, she applauded.

"Mother always enjoyed my music too," he said. His gaze strayed to a door just off the music room. "You would have liked her."

Ellen followed his gaze. "Where does that door lead?"

"Once Mother fell ill, she needed to rest often. She didn't like being confined to her bedroom, so she rested in there instead. It's a small room, but she said she enjoyed listening to the music. So she'd go in there, and I'd play the piano..." He trailed off.

"I'm sorry."

"It's fine. There are just many memories here."

"This is such a large mansion," she said, both to continue her mission and bolster his spirits. "There must be countless rooms I haven't seen yet."

Some of his spirit returned, and he jumped to his feet. "Yes, there are. Please, follow me."

They left the music room behind, and Walter continued his tour of the mansion. There were many parlors and guest rooms to keep track of, although they had yet to find the one she was most curious about, the one beneath Gerald's office. Aside from the servants, she hadn't seen anyone else in the house, and if he deplored parties, she couldn't help but wonder what they used all the space for.

"—and down here you'll find the library," Walter said, as they strode past a closed door and continued toward a large set of double doors at the end of the hall.

Ellen paused by the door they skipped. "What's in here?"

"Ah, that's just a room for the servants. Nothing too interesting. Heaven knows we have enough servants. Sometimes I think Father considers the two of us to be helpless."

She chuckled and followed him toward the library. Good to know there was a servants' room, just in case she needed it. However, her plans were starting to come together already. Gerald's office, the parlor, and the music room might be all she needed.

Nevertheless, it was good to have a contingency plan. Her years as the Domino Lady taught her that even the best-laid plans sometimes had flaws.

The library was beautiful, and from there they returned to the entrance hall and crossed to the opposite hall.

"And here is one of our finest parlors, which—" He opened the door onto a beautiful room marred by a shattered vase that had spilled dirt all over the carpeting. Two servants were cleaning up the mess. He quickly shut it again. "Ah, let's not disturb them."

"What happened?" Ellen asked.

"I assume someone knocked over one of the plants Father insists on having around. The servants will take care of it."

Her mind flashed back to the incident in the office. "Ah, so that must be what the commotion was about."

"Commotion?"

"We heard noises. Your father said they came from a parlor below."

"Ah yes, that would be it." Walter made a low sound of annoyance and shook his head. "I have told the servants to keep that window shut until a solution is found, but they seem incapable of remembering."

Then he didn't realize his father actually took advantage of the situation and preferred it this way? Ellen refrained from mentioning that.

Instead, she said, "Is there a pleasant view from the parlor? Perhaps that is why they don't remember to keep it shut."

"If you like gardens." From the tone of his voice, Walter did not.

Normally, Ellen tried to align with Walter on interests to ensure he continued to cooperate with her, but she needed an excuse to see the grounds. This was almost too perfect. "I love gardens!" She clasped her hands together, wrist bag held in a trembling grip. "I didn't know you had a garden."

Walter blinked, apparently taken aback, but then he smiled. "Why, yes, we do. Father insisted. Would you like to see it?"

"Yes, please."

"Then come right this way."

He led her back to the antechamber and then outside into the fresh air, where a cool breeze lifted her hair and blew it back from her face. She drew a deep breath and followed him around the side of the house.

A cobblestone path led them down the lawn, with large stone statues of knights to guard their progress. Ellen commented on everything they passed, the image of a girl dazzled by the sights around her. Walter's earlier consternation passed.

A cobblestone path led them down the lawn...

At last, they reached a small gate that led to a garden filled with the most beautiful flowers Ellen ever saw. Flowers of all sizes and colors bloomed in the garden, from roses to exotic plants she didn't have a name for. The path led through the garden, allowing her to fully enjoy the brilliant display of lush leaves and vibrant petals.

"They're beautiful!" As she cooed over the flowers in delight, she turned slowly to take in the full view of the garden, as well as the windows closest to it.

One window near the garden had a hint of motion inside. When she focused on it, she could make out the silhouettes of the servants as they cleaned up the fallen vase. That was the parlor, in which case, the window above it on the second floor had to be Gerald's office.

The wall beneath the window was unfortunately smooth, with nothing that might grant a would-be climber a way to reach the second floor. Further down, though, past the garden, vines curled along a high trellis that looked sturdy enough to support her slight frame.

A plan slowly took shape in the little adventuress's mind.

"I'm pleased you like it," Walter said. "Gardening has never been my thing, but I suppose everyone has different tastes."

"It's wonderful. Thank you for showing me. The flowers are so beautiful."

"They're not nearly as beautiful as you." He crouched and plucked a rose from the nearest bush. He held it out. "You are a flower far lovelier than anything grown in a garden."

Ellen accepted the rose with a blush and held it against her chest. "You flatter me too much."

"I can't help it. You are like no one I've ever met before."

She laughed and waved off his compliment.

Walter took a step closer. "Of all the girls I've met at all the occasions Father took me to, never before have I met someone as enchanting and delightful as you. You are truly special, Ellen Patrick."

Then he kissed her.

At first, Ellen gasped, startled, but then she relaxed into his embrace. His strong arms awoke desires within her, and she reflected with sorrow that romance had no place in her life. While she devoted her free time to many things and enjoyed social outings with friends, marriage and a family were too dangerous for someone in her line of work. And she refused to abandon her goal until the corrupt system had been destroyed—a job that might last a lifetime.

But for the moment, she enjoyed the kiss in the garden, surrounded by beautiful flowers, and dreamed of a future that would never be hers.

A few days later, Ellen once again joined Walter in the mansion antechamber. "Thank you for having me."

"Did I not make my interest clear enough the last time?" he asked with a teasing smile.

She returned his smile with a coy flutter of her eyelashes. "Perhaps not."

Walter kissed her again, as he had in the garden, then stepped back and placed his hands on her arms. "You are welcome here any time, my dear. And every time I see you, it seems you become more beautiful."

She blushed under his gaze. She wore a long blue gown that shimmered as she walked, and a thick black shawl covered her pale shoulders.

"I worried," she said, "that with what the newspapers have been saying, you wouldn't want company."

For the newspapers had exploded with the news that Gerald Wilson received a letter from the mysterious Domino Lady, warning him that if he didn't confess to his wrongdoings, the masked vigilante would see to it herself that justice was done. It had already brought Gerald's role as a political boss into the light, while everyone bandied gossip about what ill deeds the Domino Lady might mean.

Walter shook his head. "You mean those threats? Bah, there's nothing to her accusations."

"Even so, if she believes there is—"

"No woman, even one with her reputation, has the power to harm my father." He threw back his head and laughed. "Even if this so-called 'Domino Lady' had the skill to reach him, there is nothing to uncover. An innocent man has no reason to back down in the face of blackmail."

"Oh, I didn't mean to imply he should! I just worried for him... and for you."

"Think nothing of it," Walter said. "The mansion is well-guarded, and I will protect you if anything happens. You are perfectly safe with me."

"Thank you."

"Now, come. Our dinner is waiting."

Ellen extended one dainty hand to Walter and let him escort her into the dining room, where the table was set for two.

"Where does your father eat?" she asked.

"Father is odd about these things. He eats alone in a private room down the hall from his office."

She'd observed the mansion from a distance several times since their meeting and noticed that there was a time every evening around dinnertime when Gerald's office went dark, only for the lamp to go on again approximately two hours later. At the time, she assumed he had dinner with Walter, but apparently not. Still, the timing would work for her purposes—perhaps even better than in her original plan.

They spoke of simple matters over dinner, while Ellen thought through her next steps. She hoped to find definitive evidence in Gerald's office, but if she couldn't, Walter would have to act as her proxy.

If Walter Wilson went to the police, they would be unable to ignore it unless they found a way to silence him, and what she'd seen of Gerald's affection for him made it unlikely he would go to such extremes. It was a gamble, but a promising one.

When they finished their meal, they went together to the parlor below Gerald's office, where the open window offered a clear view of the garden. Ellen sank onto the couch, and Walter sat beside her.

"It's a beautiful night out," she said.

"All the more beautiful with you here."

She laughed. "You flatter me too much."

"Never enough."

They sat together in the parlor for some time, but just as Ellen began to prepare an excuse to go elsewhere, Walter cleared his throat.

"I have been working on something special for you. Would you care to see it now?"

"A surprise?"

"Yes. It's in the music room."

"I'd love to."

Ellen stood and offered Walter her arm. He placed his hand on her elbow and they left the parlor. He never looked back to notice the wrist bag she abandoned between the cushions.

In the music room, he sat at the piano. "I wrote this song in your honor. I call it 'Beautiful Maiden.'"

Though the title was somewhat uninspired, the music was not. It was a smooth, simple melody that brought to mind delicate beauty, like a fragile bird or butterfly, beauty that might be lost in a moment if not treated with gentleness and care.

As Ellen listened, she smiled. If Walter only knew the sort of song that would truly suit her, a song of adventure and intrigue hidden behind the mask.

But although she wanted to enjoy the music, the clock was ticking. She stood, as if in sudden alarm, and lifted a hand to her forehead. "Walter—"

"What is it?"

"The music is beautiful, truly, but I..." She took a step and lurched forward in an affected stumble. "I don't feel well."

"Ellen!" He jumped to his feet. "Are you all right?"

"Yes, I..."

She let herself sway again, and he caught her. "Do you need a doctor?"

"I don't think so. I think I just need some rest... I should probably go home." Ellen reached toward the chair and made a show of looking around it with increasing confusion. "My wrist bag, I've lost it!"

"What? How is that possible?"

"I must have left it in the dining room or parlor earlier."

"I'll go retrieve it for you." Walter's brow furrowed. "Yet I hardly want to leave you alone when you aren't feeling well."

"It's not that bad."

"Yes, but if you fell and I wasn't here to help—"

"I do feel a little faint," she said, in the reluctant tone of someone who didn't want to admit to her weaknesses so readily. "Is there somewhere I could lie down?"

For the little room adjacent to the music chamber was ideal for her plan, far enough from the parlor to buy the time she needed. She waited. It had to be Walter's idea if possible, or he might get suspicious.

"You can rest in the next room," he said, "while I look for your wrist bag."

"Thank you."

He led her into the room, and she settled down on the couch where his mother once must have rested.

"Are you sure you're feeling all right?" he asked. "I can call a doctor."

"I don't need a doctor, as long as you care for me."

That earned a smile.

She rubbed her head. "But please, close the door so the servants won't disturb me."

"As you wish. I'll knock when I return. Do you know if you had the bag in the parlor?"

"I'm afraid I can't remember. I'm sorry."

"All right. I won't take long."

The moment the door closed behind him, Ellen sat up and went into action. First she stripped off the blue gown she wore, for beneath it was the form-fitting white gown of the Domino Lady. As for her shawl, it unfolded to reveal its true form, a black silk cape she slung across her shoulders. From a hidden pocket within its folds, she retrieved her black domino mask.

Another hidden pocket contained her trusted automatic, as well as a few more surprises in case they became necessary to use.

Ellen dashed to the window and opened it. She was outside in an instant, not daring to waste any time. She had to get to Gerald's office before Walter reached the parlor. The dining room was closer, so he should check it first, but then he'd be on his way.

She took the shortest path around the mansion grounds at a run, until she reached the trellis in the garden. It afforded her access to the second floor, and she forced her way inside with the help of the jimmy she'd placed with the rest of her equipment. Inside, the hallway was empty. If she'd timed things correctly and the usual pattern held, Gerald would soon be heading back to his office.

The office door was unlocked. No one was inside yet. Ellen slipped in and closed the door behind her.

First, she opened the window. That would allow Walter to play the role she had in mind. Next, she turned her attention to Gerald's desk. It had two drawers, both locked, but they were minor obstacles thanks to hairpins she'd worn for the occasion.

Within the drawers, she found a goldmine of information. Gerald had added blackmailing to his repertoire of shady deals, if the stack of cash in one drawer was any indication. Ellen slipped the money into a large pocket of her cape. Far better for it to be donated to people in need than to fund further corruption.

Most of the rest were letters. They showed the strings Gerald pulled across the city and deals he made—and then she spied the one she needed, a letter from an anonymous associate warning Gerald that Daniel was starting to suspect him.

Ellen claimed the packet of letters and slipped them into her cape as well. In their place, she set down a small card that read "The Domino Lady's Compliments!" She also found a blank sheet of paper and placed it on top of the desk.

Then she drew her automatic and waited.

While the documents appeared damning to her, they weren't enough.

If the police were unwilling to pursue the leads presented by Daniel's journal, they would be just as reluctant to follow up on this. No doubt they would claim it was circumstantial evidence. Motive and lack of an alibi notwithstanding, she had no definitive proof that Gerald was the murderer.

That left only one option: a confession.

If she'd misjudged the timing, this would become much more difficult. Her heart hammered. A sudden creak met her ears through the open window, and she held her breath. That had to be the parlor door opening. Walter was in position.

Gerald had to come soon. Of all days for him to have a longer dinner!

Footsteps in the hall signaled his return. Perfect timing after all. She braced herself, gun at the ready. When the door opened and the political boss stepped in, she leveled her weapon at him. "Freeze! Get your hands in the air."

His eyes widened, and he flinched. His gaze darted toward the hall.

"Don't even think about running or I'll blow a hole in your head!" With the gun trained on him, she beckoned him closer. "Shut the door."

Gerald took a slow step forward and closed the door behind him. He lifted his hands in the air. "You won't get away with this."

"I already am."

"I don't know how you got in here past my security, but you'll never get off the grounds."

Her laugh was harsh. "I have my ways. You should be more concerned about yourself."

"You're the Domino Lady."

"That's right. And if you know that much, then you know why I'm here."

He wet his lips. "You want me to confess."

"Yes." She gestured toward the blank sheet of paper on the desk. "Confess everything. Now!"

"They'll never believe me if I confess under coercion. I'll say you forced me to lie."

"I've already taken the documents that will support your words." And if everything had gone according to plan, she had a witness listening in. There was no way Walter could have heard the start of their conversation without stopping to eavesdrop. He should still be in the parlor, listening at the window as the notorious Domino Lady confronted his father. And if he raced upstairs instead, she would force him to hear the confession—at gunpoint, if necessary. "You've had your hands in every shady dealing this city has seen for years."

Gerald lifted his chin, a glimmer of pride restored to his features despite his hands in the air. "I wouldn't expect a woman like you to understand what I've done."

"I understand better than you do. I understand that people with authority are meant to use it for the good of the people, not for the good of themselves. Your primary goal was lining your own pockets. Bribery, blackmail..."

"I did what I had to do!"

"You *had* to do those things? Don't make me laugh."

"The world is a cruel place." His lip curled into a sneer. "Someone who dons a black mask to break into houses and holds people at gunpoint is hardly in a position to criticize me."

"I work to help those who need it. You only worked to help yourself."

He scowled. "I refuse to be judged by a vigilante!"

"Then let the police judge you. I'm still waiting for you to write your confession."

"But—"

She cocked her gun. "Would you rather I deliver your corpse to the police instead?"

"No! I'm going, I'm going."

She kept the weapon trained on him as he shuffled to his desk. Alert for any tricks, she was prepared to fire if she had to, even though the Domino Lady never killed her targets. She hoped the day would never come when she had to, but it was always a grim possibility in the back of her mind.

Part of the price to pay to see that justice was served.

Gerald scribbled a few sentences, signed the paper, and then shoved it toward her. "There. Are you satisfied?"

Without taking her eyes from him, she snatched up the piece of paper. "Keep your hands in the air."

He swallowed hard and obeyed.

Ellen read over the confession. Although short, it covered the basics. He explained his position as a corrupt political boss, admitted to using bribery and blackmail to get what he wanted, and even named the men he kept in power through such dubious means.

But that was it.

"You forgot one thing," she said.

"What?"

"Daniel Ambrose."

His eyes widened. "How do you know about that?"

"I have my ways."

"Is that what this is about? Who sent you?"

"You're not in any position to be asking questions."

"Do you expect me to confess to murder?"

"Your choice." She aimed her gun. "You could die here."

"Was that the plan all along?" he asked "Was I always set up to be the scapegoat, after everything I've done?"

She narrowed her eyes. "What are you babbling about?"

At first, Gerald stared at her, but then he started to laugh. "You weren't in on it, were you? You actually believe what you're saying. Let me guess, he told you I was the murderer and asked you to force me into a confession?"

Ellen hadn't expected it to be easy to get him to confess, but most people became more cooperative with a gun pointed at them. Yet despite confessing to the other crimes when threatened, he continued to profess innocence in regards to the murder.

None of the evidence she found confirmed anything except that Gerald knew Daniel had uncovered evidence of his corruption. Either his sudden claim of innocence was a ploy because he knew she didn't have anything definite...

...or Gerald Wilson wasn't the murderer after all.

Ellen had heard many confessions since she became the Domino Lady. She was used to criminals making up stories and feigning innocence. Something in Gerald's voice didn't sound quite right. This wasn't the return of his earlier bravado, but desperation mixed with righteous fury.

It sounded like the truth.

"Talk," she snapped, her voice clipped and terse. "If you didn't kill Ambrose, who did?"

He hesitated.

"Don't play dumb. Calling yourself a scapegoat, asking if 'he' accused you; you know who the real murderer is and you're going to tell me if you don't want to be riddled with lead."

Still he didn't speak.

"You're guilty of covering up a murder at the very least! Do you really want that to be the legacy you leave to the world?"

"My legacy." As if the word triggered something in him, he sneered. "Oh yes, I'm leaving quite a legacy behind, aren't I? A history of crimes, a cover-up, and a murderer." He let out a bitter laugh. "A murderer whose crime I'll be blamed for if you have your way. What a legacy."

A murderer as his legacy?

Suspicion clenched Ellen's heart in a vice, but she kept her face emotionless. "I want a name."

"Perhaps I shouldn't have covered it up… perhaps I've been trying too hard… All these years, I thought there was a way out…"

"Enough! I don't have time for your self-pitying introspection."

Gerald met her gaze. He no longer looked angry, just sad.

"Who killed Daniel Ambrose?"

"My son," he said. "Walter."

Truth rang through his words.

Ellen uttered an unladylike curse and raced for the door. She had to get back into position immediately. She couldn't afford to get there late.

Because Walter had heard his father's confession, and if Ellen didn't keep her cover intact, it might be curtains for the Domino Lady.

At the bottom of the trellis, Ellen allowed herself a brief pause to hide her automatic within one of her cape's pockets before she started running. She couldn't afford stealth this time. The clock was ticking.

In her original plan, it didn't matter too much if she was late. As long as she returned to the room before Walter did, she could feign a reason why she wasn't ready for him to come in yet if he knocked while she was still changing out of her costume. He'd struck her as too much of a gentleman to barge in when a lady asked him not to.

But she'd misjudged him, and dangerously so. Any delay or excuse would surely be a warning sign to him, if he'd indeed overheard the confrontation and knew the Domino Lady had learned his identity.

It almost made her laugh. When she developed this plan, Walter overhearing his father's confession was critical. He was to be the witness she needed. In the end, it would have been much better if he remained oblivious to the entire thing.

She sprinted to the window she'd left open and peeked into the room where she was supposed to be "resting." Empty. So far, so good. She climbed back inside and stripped out of the white frock as fast as she could, no longer trusting to keep it hidden under her blue gown. She wrapped her domino mask in the white silk and dropped them on the floor.

From a tiny pocket in her cape, she withdrew a small vial of liquid. If anyone saw it, it would look like some sort of clear nail polish, but woe to the unwary fool who tasted it. It was in fact a potent acid, one that served the Domino Lady well. She dumped it onto the telltale dress and mask, which she'd treated beforehand with a special chemical. Within seconds, they would be reduced to black ash.

She pulled on her blue gown and then folded up her cape. After a few careful adjustments, it once again appeared to be a thick shawl, which she arranged around her shoulders.

On the floor, only ash remained. She scooped it up and dumped it into one of the many potted plants Gerald so loved. It blended perfectly with the dirt. Then she shut the window and took a breath to compose herself.

A knock came at the door. "Ellen?" Tension disrupted Walter's normally-calm voice.

Ellen ran a hand through her hair to make sure it wasn't too mussed from her mad dash around the mansion and arranged herself on the couch the way he left her.

The knock came more sharply. "Are you in there?"

"Walter?" She spoke slowly, pitching her voice as if she'd just woken up. "Come in."

He burst into the room and frowned at her, eyes narrowed with suspicion.

She sat up and blinked, again feigning tiredness. "You were gone so long, I must have fallen asleep." She yawned and ran her fingers through her curls again. "Did you find my bag?"

"What? Oh, yes." He held out the wrist bag, but continued to stare at her.

More grateful than ever for her precautions, she accepted it and stood up. Unless he guessed the secret of her shawl, he'd realize she couldn't be hiding the Domino Lady's supplies and stolen documents on her person. And after all, he'd had her wrist bag during the incident.

Walter's shoulders relaxed. "Did you see anyone through the window?"

"No." She blinked. "Why? What happened?"

"That woman, the Domino Lady. She was here."

Ellen drew a sharp breath. "The Domino Lady? What did she do? Is your father all right?"

"He's fine, but we'll need to figure things out. I'm sorry, Ellen, I'd hoped to spend more time together this evening, but we'll have to say good night now."

"I understand. I hope everything works out."

Walter reached out to her. "You're feeling better, I assume?"

"Yes, much better."

He burst into the room…

As he walked her back through the mansion to the main entrance, she tried to figure him out. It was horrible to think that this soft-spoken, seemingly plain gentleman was the sort of ruthless murderer who had killed Daniel.

A murderer in the guise of a gentleman and a vigilante behind a lady's façade. What a pair they made.

In the antechamber, Walter looked into her eyes. "Good night."

"Good night."

She managed not to shudder when he kissed her.

The next day, Ellen lounged in a silk kimono while reading a book, a bit of relaxation in celebration of her victory. By now, the police would have received the parcel left for them, and within it, the documents she'd claimed from Gerald's desk—as well as a note from the Domino Lady, informing them that Gerald had covered up the murder for his son.

Despite the unexpected surprise, Walter's role actually worked in her favor. The police hesitated to take down a powerful political boss, but they'd have fewer qualms about convicting a young businessman. It might even let them paint Gerald's corruption in a sympathetic light so they could wash their hands of the whole affair.

Meanwhile, the proceeds obtained from Gerald's ill dealings were on their way to a charitable cause, courtesy of the Domino Lady.

The telephone rang.

Ellen stretched, set down her book, and picked up the phone. "Hello?" she asked, her voice kept at a soft, emotional pitch until she knew who was on the other end.

"Ellen?" Nancy asked. "Have you heard the news?"

"What news?"

"Gerald Wilson murdered Daniel."

Ellen sat straight up. "What's this all about?"

"The police just told me. I imagine it will be all over the city soon."

Impossible. They were set on ignoring Gerald and finding someone else to blame. Why would they accept the Domino Lady's evidence against him but ignore her message about Walter?

"He didn't seem like a murderer," she said, with no need to feign her confusion. "Are they sure it was him?"

"Apparently they received a message from the Domino Lady—you know, that vigilante who threatened him, the one all the newspapers were talking about?—and when they went to the Wilson mansion to follow up on it, they found…" Her voice cracked.

A cold chill swept over Ellen. "What? What did they find when they went to the mansion?"

"Oh Ellen, it's terrible. Gerald Wilson had written a note confessing to the murder, and then he killed himself."

How could someone appear so calm and rational, yet be so cold-blooded? Ellen regarded Walter with a bit of fascination as she entered the mansion for his father's wake, dressed in a long black dress for mourning.

"Thank you for coming," he said, his tone morose. "I know Father had become fond of you."

Ellen inclined her head in acknowledgement and tried not to let her emotions show. There were only two plausible possibilities. Either Gerald had lied to her and felt guilty enough to kill himself after the fact—unlikely—or Walter murdered him and made it look like suicide after she left that night. Considering Gerald's demeanor during his confession and Walter's reaction afterwards, it was the latter, yet to all appearances, he looked like he was truly grieving.

"I'm sorry for your loss," she said.

"Thank you." Walter shook his head. "This has all been such a shock."

Ellen nodded, placed her hand on his arm in a gesture of sympathy, and then moved on. Thank goodness as the only living family member, he had to greet everyone as they arrived. If she was trapped by his side the entire time and had to develop another ploy to get away, he might become too suspicious.

Although she was there on a mission, she began by paying her respects to Gerald's memory. Ever since the revelation in his office, she'd wondered how corrupt he actually was. The line had become blurry. Where did Walter's actions stop and his begin? His comments suggested he did more than just cover up the murder for him. Were his political machinations for his own benefit or his son's?

Ellen moved on and entered polite conversation with various guests she remembered from Nancy's party. Once some time had passed, she casually asked one of them, "By the way, do you know why Walter wants us to gather in the library at two o'clock?"

The other woman blinked. "I didn't know he did."

"Oh?" Ellen feigned surprise and gestured vaguely toward some of the other groups she'd been talking to. "They were discussing it over there."

"Really? Well, thank you for letting me know. I don't know what it's about, but I'll keep it in mind."

Still in the guise of questioning the strange instruction, Ellen mentioned it to several more people. When a man approached and passed on the same message to her, she thanked him with an inward smile of triumph. She'd done her job. Word was spreading—everyone heard it from someone else that Walter wanted them in the library at two.

Heading to the library would take them right past the secret room, a precaution in case things grew dangerous.

After so many visits to the mansion, it was an easy matter to casually slip into the hall and find an unoccupied parlor. There, Ellen removed the outer layer of her black funeral dress to reveal its true form—her other costume as the Domino Lady! This one a black backless crepe dress of her own design, its material clung close to her shapely form. From within the folds of the black silk that had served as a wider skirt just moments ago, she retrieved a piece of cloth that unfolded into a contrasting white cape. She fastened it about her neck, and then she put on her black domino mask.

Trusty automatic in hand, she crept out of the parlor and made her way through the mansion toward the room Walter had refused her entry to during his tour. Though he claimed it was merely a room for the servants, he showed no such secrecy about the others. It was the one room he never let her see. Something had to be in there.

She'd once again brought her folding jimmy, which made short work of the lock. Ellen glanced around to make sure the hall was empty and then opened the door. She had approximately half an hour before the guests would head to the "gathering" in the library. Even if some of them learned that Walter never made such a request, surely at least a few would go there.

Darkness obscured the room. To her surprise, she realized it had no windows. Light from the hall helped her find the lamp, and she turned it on. The inconsequential room turned out to be an office. Walter's office, no doubt.

She shut the door behind her.

For all the secrecy, the office looked plain enough. Like its owner, it appeared geared toward business. No plants like those that sat in Gerald's office, no photographs or even hints of opulence, just gray cabinets in the far corners and a wooden desk at the center. Even the lamp was as plain as could be, built for functionality rather than decoration.

Ellen scanned the room for any sign of traps, then crept to the desk.

The top was entirely bare, but it had six drawers, three on each side. A quick inspection showed that all of them were protected with intricate locks. She briefly considered a search for the keys, but abandoned it. Most likely Walter carried them with him; he certainly wouldn't hide them in the same room as the locks. So she set down her gun and went to work.

As in Gerald's office, she used hairpins to work on the desk's small locks. They were tricky, even for someone experienced. Walter must have bought top-notch equipment to guard his secrets. Ellen took a deep breath and worked with caution. Once the first lock opened, she resisted the urge to yank the drawer open and instead examined it.

Sure enough, she found a slight catch at the edge. Its purpose was unclear, but it would be triggered if the drawer was opened. No doubt it would set off an alarm or otherwise alert Walter to the break-in.

Ellen took another breath to steady herself and studied the trap so she could figure out how to bypass it. Her heart hammered with the thrill of adventure. Never had she faced such obstacles. The added challenge heightened the tension, as any mistake could doom her.

At last, she slid the catch to the side so that the drawer could be safely opened. The papers inside painted a chilling picture. Without context, they were innocuous enough, just ways certain politicians and other powerful figures had lent support to Walter's business.

But she recognized the names, the names of the men Gerald put into power. Her earlier suspicions settled into certainty. The late political boss no longer seemed like a sinister figure so much as a puppet being controlled from the shadows.

After a cursory glance through the papers to make sure they were what they appeared to be, Ellen moved onto the next drawer.

Another lock and another trap, all while the clock ticked down. The young adventuress was far too aware that if she didn't find what she needed soon, her plans might be for nothing. She'd never get another opportunity like this without arousing Walter's suspicions.

The second drawer contained personal papers. So he did keep such things in his office after all, if only a few. Ellen nearly moved on, but one at the bottom of the pile caught her eye. It was a handwritten note, written in lovely curling letters, and it was addressed to Gerald.

Unable to resist her curiosity, she read it. The letter came from Walter's mother. In it, she expressed her fear to Gerald that she didn't have long to live, chastised him for not spending enough time with his family, and asked him to promise that he be there for their son once she was gone.

So that was it. Ellen's heart ached for them in a way she never thought possible for people involved in such corruption. She'd wondered how Walter could have controlled his father. She'd wondered why Gerald, who seemed to have no qualms about anything, would cover up a murder for his son. She'd assumed it had to be blackmail of some kind, but she couldn't fathom how.

Perhaps it wasn't blackmail, but a nightmarish twisting of family affection, a dying request from his sickly wife that Walter held over his head for all these years.

The documents might be enough. Ellen glanced at the remaining locked drawers and hesitated. All she needed was to make the connection apparent. The police should still have the message from the Domino Lady claiming Walter was the murderer; proof of the benefits Walter personally received from his father's machinations might be enough for them to investigate Gerald's suicide. And the longer she spent in the office, the more likely it was she'd be caught—and that Ellen Patrick's disappearance from the wake would be noticed.

She reached for the documents in the first drawer.

A quiet *click* of the doorknob was her only warning. Someone was about to enter. She held her breath. It had to be Walter.

There was nowhere in the room she could hide, unless she remained crouched under the desk, and given the lack of furniture in the office, that was likely the first place he'd go whether he was searching for an intruder or not. So instead, she retrieved her gun, straightened up, and aimed at the door.

It opened.

Bang!

The noise came first and then the pain. Ellen's automatic dropped from her bloody fingers. It happened so fast, it took her a moment to catch up. She looked at the blood on her hand and then up at Walter, who stepped into his office with a gun in his hand, his demeanor as calm as if this sort of thing happened all the time.

The truth settled onto her with a cold chill. He'd entered the office expecting her, and he shot the moment he saw her.

"Don't move," he said, as she reached for her fallen gun. "I'll kill you."

She froze and thought through her options. Diving behind the desk would give her a moment of cover. With her right hand injured, she wouldn't be able to shoot as well, but at least she'd have a chance. Walter wasn't bluffing, but she doubted he'd let her live if she cooperated, either.

It was visible in his eyes, the ruthlessness she hadn't been able to reconcile with him before. He looked dispassionate, almost unconcerned, but equally merciless. There hadn't been a trace of emotion in his face when he shot her. No matter what she did, he'd kill her in a heartbeat, just as he'd killed his father.

So Ellen dropped behind the desk and grabbed her fallen gun. A bullet struck the desk above her.

Walter's voice was quiet. It would have sounded almost gentle if she didn't know better. "You might think I won't want to make noise with so many guests here who might find us. But when they see what happened, everyone will understand that I had to defend myself against the Domino Lady, especially after she drove Father to commit suicide."

Gun in hand, Ellen peeked out from behind the desk. She didn't want to kill him, but if she could wound him or even force him to drop the gun like he'd done to her, she could regain the upper hand.

Another shot struck the edge of the desk seconds after she pulled herself back behind cover. Her heart pounded from fear, but also excitement. Even though blood trickled down her hand, adrenaline dulled the pain. Yes, there was a certain thrill to a confrontation that put her life on the line and her skill to the test.

"You killed him, didn't you?" she asked. "You killed your own father."

"The truth doesn't matter. All that matters is what people see. I knew you would come here to find evidence."

Footsteps. Walter was approaching the desk. Ellen carefully set down her automatic. With the desk shielding her, he couldn't see what she was doing. She reached into the bodice of her dress, where she'd hidden a tiny hypodermic needle filled with a potent but non-lethal tranquilizer. She concealed it in the palm of her uninjured hand.

"You think you're pretty clever," Walter said, as his voice and footsteps drew nearer. "You fancy yourself some sort of justice-dealing vigilante, a hero who can expose corruption and root out evildoers. Now look at you. Hiding as you wait for death to arrive. You're no hero, Domino Lady."

Ellen didn't dare look out to see how close he was. She needed to wait until the right moment.

"I've spent years covering my tracks. Father was the perfect front. He never could deny me anything after Mother died."

"You're a monster."

He laughed, but there was hardly any emotion in it. "Is that how you see it? Odd, for a vigilante to see things in such shades of black and white. You think the world owes you something, so you take things by force. I'm the same way. When Mother died, I vowed that I would make the most out of my life—without endangering myself."

Closer. Closer. Just a little longer.

"I've taken great care to cultivate my image over the years. Everyone thinks I'm quiet and mild-mannered, even a bit dull, a man who lacks imagination. That's fine by me. I don't need fame or glory. I have everything I want."

Ellen held her breath.

Another footstep. Any minute and he'd be in position to shoot her dead, but if she moved too soon, he'd have a clear shot. She tensed—now!

As Walter reached the side of the desk, she leaped out of hiding and tackled him. With her bloody hand, she tried to force his gun away, while she swung the hidden needle toward him with the other. Taken by surprise, he lost his grip on the gun. It fell to the floor. At the same time, however, he caught her wrists.

She closed her fist around the hypodermic again. He hadn't seen it. If he didn't notice, it could still be her way to victory. She struggled against his greater strength, as if her only plan had been take his weapon or run away.

"You think you're so clever," he said. He pinned her against him. His eyes were cold. "But in the end, you're just a foolish girl."

"Why did you kill your father?" she asked. "Answer me!"

"Because he was going to betray me. You put pressure on him, and when the police showed up, he would have told them everything."

"So you killed him." She snorted. "Now you don't have him to cover for you."

"True. You've been quite an obstacle to my plans." His gaze slid across her pinned body. "An attractive obstacle, though."

As he slid his hand around the front of her dress, she tensed.

"This is the end for you, Domino Lady."

Footsteps and distant voices came from the hall. The guests on their way to the library, just as she'd planned.

"No," she said. "Not for me."

Ellen slammed her fist into his leg, releasing the tranquilizer into his system. His grip on her broke and she wrenched herself free from his weakening gasp. Mouth open in disbelief, he sank to the floor. One hand reached toward the gun, but she kicked it out of reach.

There was enough in the office to condemn him, and he wouldn't be conscious for a long while. Ellen tossed a card that read "The Domino Lady's Compliments" onto his desk and retrieved her automatic. Then she threw his desk chair to the ground to ensure the guests outside heard the noise and investigated. Footsteps pounded toward the office.

Ellen flattened herself alongside the door and removed her mask and cape. She folded the cape and hid both within her wrist bag.

The door swung open, momentarily hiding her.

"What's going on?" one of the guests asked.

"Is that Mr. Wilson?"

"Someone call the police!"

More guests entered the office to see what was going on, and Ellen slipped out of hiding to join them. A few glanced at her, but since she was still in black, it was unlikely they'd realize her dress wasn't the same in all the confusion.

She cradled her injured hand so the blood couldn't be seen and hurried out of the office.

Whispers followed her. "She was seeing Walter, wasn't she?"

"Poor girl, she must be horrified."

"What in the world happened here?"

Ellen smiled to herself and continued back through the mansion to retrieve the discarded pieces of her mourning gown and leave the rest to the police.

"I can't believe Walter Wilson was responsible for everything," Nancy said, as they sat together drinking tea.

Ellen nodded, a somber expression fixed on her face.

"Oh—I forgot that you and he…"

"It's fine," she said. "He wasn't the man he appeared to be."

"Are you coping with the shock well enough? After I heard about your accident, I didn't know what to think."

Ellen held up her bandaged hand and laughed away her concerns. "I suppose I was a little distracted, but I'm feeling much better now." She'd had little choice but to feign an accident to explain her injury. "I'm glad I found out the truth about Walter."

"We both owe a great debt to the Domino Lady." Nancy rubbed her chin. "Vigilante or not, she must not be so bad. After all, if it wasn't for her, an innocent man would have been convicted of Daniel's murder... and you'd still be deceived by Walter. Who knows, you could be engaged to a murderer by now!"

Ellen let a light chuckle be her only answer.

"I wish there was some way we could repay her."

"You know," she said, "I've heard the Domino Lady always donates any money she takes to charity. I was thinking of selling the gifts Walter gave to me and donating the money in her honor."

Nancy clasped her hands together. "That's a wonderful idea. I could do the same thing with the money I found. It seems like Gerald was trying to buy Daniel's silence. I felt uncomfortable having it, but now I know what to do. I'll donate it to charity, for the Domino Lady."

Ellen smiled and lifted her cup. "For the Domino Lady."

The End

WRITING ABOUT THE DOMINO LADY

I'm a newcomer to pulp fiction.

Now, some of my biggest writing influences—chief among them, H.P. Lovecraft—wrote for pulp magazines, but whenever someone would ask me to explain pulp fiction, I didn't really have an answer. So when a writing conference I was attending included a presentation on the new pulp market, I knew I had to go. The presentation grabbed my attention right away. Pulp fiction's exciting, fast-paced adventures sounded like my sort of thing, and I was especially interested in the idea that new stories were being written about classic pulp heroes. I love developing stories with established characters.

There was only one thing to do after that: pick up a few pulp collections and start reading.

Among the books I bought was a collection of the original Domino Lady stories. I included it almost as an afterthought, but the writing hooked me more than the others. Instead of moving from collection to collection as I planned, I sat down and read every story about the Domino Lady.

They were fun and fast-paced, and I could tell the original writer took great delight in his heroine's love for adventure and devotion to justice. I've always enjoyed characters that plan out and enact a perfect scheme, and the Domino Lady delivered, always having a clever way to get the job done while concealing her identity. I also enjoyed how her behavior changed depending on which role she was in. In her normal day-to-day life, Ellen Patrick plays into people's expectations about her—we're talking about a character who intentionally puts a "peculiarly emotional quiver" into her voice when talking to certain people—but when she confronts her enemies as the Domino Lady, she's harsh, threatening, and in command.

After I finished the collection, I kept thinking about her. Soon, a story idea took shape in my mind. She'd be hunting for a murderer, and she'd find a way to force the murderer into a confession that someone else would overhear.

I wanted it to *feel* like a Domino Lady story despite not having the same writing style as the originals, which posed a problem. In the end, I decided to blend the two and write the story in my normal style while also including certain phrases and descriptions the originals favored.

Within a few days, I was writing the story idea that would become "The Domino Lady Takes the Case."

Or at least, half of it.

My original idea didn't include the twist. I wrote the majority of the story just as I'd envisioned it, but as I approached the confession scene, it felt too straightforward and predictable. As much as I loved the Domino Lady carrying her plan out perfectly... what if she was *wrong*?

A different scene took shape in my mind, and I wrote it. Suddenly, the story wasn't over, the killer hadn't been caught. She needed a new plan—and so did I, because I hadn't figured out how she would overcome these new odds.

That set me back a bit, but I worked out a new direction for the remainder of the story to take and edited the earlier scenes with it in mind. The result is here, and I think the story is better for it.

Did it work out well? I'll let you be the judge. Either way, I had fun writing about the Domino Lady and hope to return to her in the future.

SAMANTHA LIENHARD has been writing for most of her life, especially in the fantasy and horror genres. She graduated from Mansfield University with a B.A. in English and a minor in Creative Writing, and then from Seton Hill University with an M.F.A. in Writing Popular Fiction. When she isn't writing, she can usually be found playing video games.

Her publications include a comedy novella called *The Zombie Mishap*, a Lovecraftian horror novella called *The Book at Dernier*, a Lovecraftian horror novelette called *It Came Back*, and several short horror stories.

She also writes for video games and has worked on the scripts for several indie titles, including *Ascendant Hearts*, *The Trials of Olympus III*, *My Devil Girlfriend*, and *Eternal Radiance*.

Information about all of her work can be found at her website: http://www.samanthalienhard.com